New England
Tall Tales & White Lies

Other books from Peterbrook Publishing Society:

NEW ENGLAND COUNTRY STORE COOKBOOK

IN THE DAY OF THE LORD
The Exciting and Promised Fulfillment of the Good News
Unveiled in Revelation

THE SONS OF PATRIOTS

SELLING YOURSELF AS A SCRIPTWRITER
IN HOLLYWOOD
A 12-step Marketing Plan for New & Used Screenwriters

*Available from Amazon.com and
from booksellers worldwide.*

New England Tall Tales & White Lies

Peter W. Smith

Illustrations by Paule Loring

The Peterbrook Publishing Society
Concord, New Hampshire USA

New England Tall Tales & White Lies

© 2005 by Peter W. Smith except the Paule Loring drawings,
which are © by Virginia Loring and used by permission.
All Rights Reserved.

No part of this book may be reproduced or transmitted in any form or by
any means, graphic, electronic or mechanical including photocopying,
recording, taping or by any information storage or retrieval system,
except for brief quotations in critical reviews,
without permission in writing from the publisher.

The places, names, and situations in these stories are
entirely fictional, and any resemblance to persons
living or dead is coincidental and unintended.

The Peterbrook Publishing Society
Post Office Box 140
Concord, New Hampshire 03302 USA
peterbrook@mail.com

ISBN: 1-4196-5726-7

Printed in the United States of America

Never go out to meet trouble.
If you will just sit still, nine cases out of ten
someone will intercept it
before it reaches you.

Calvin Coolidge

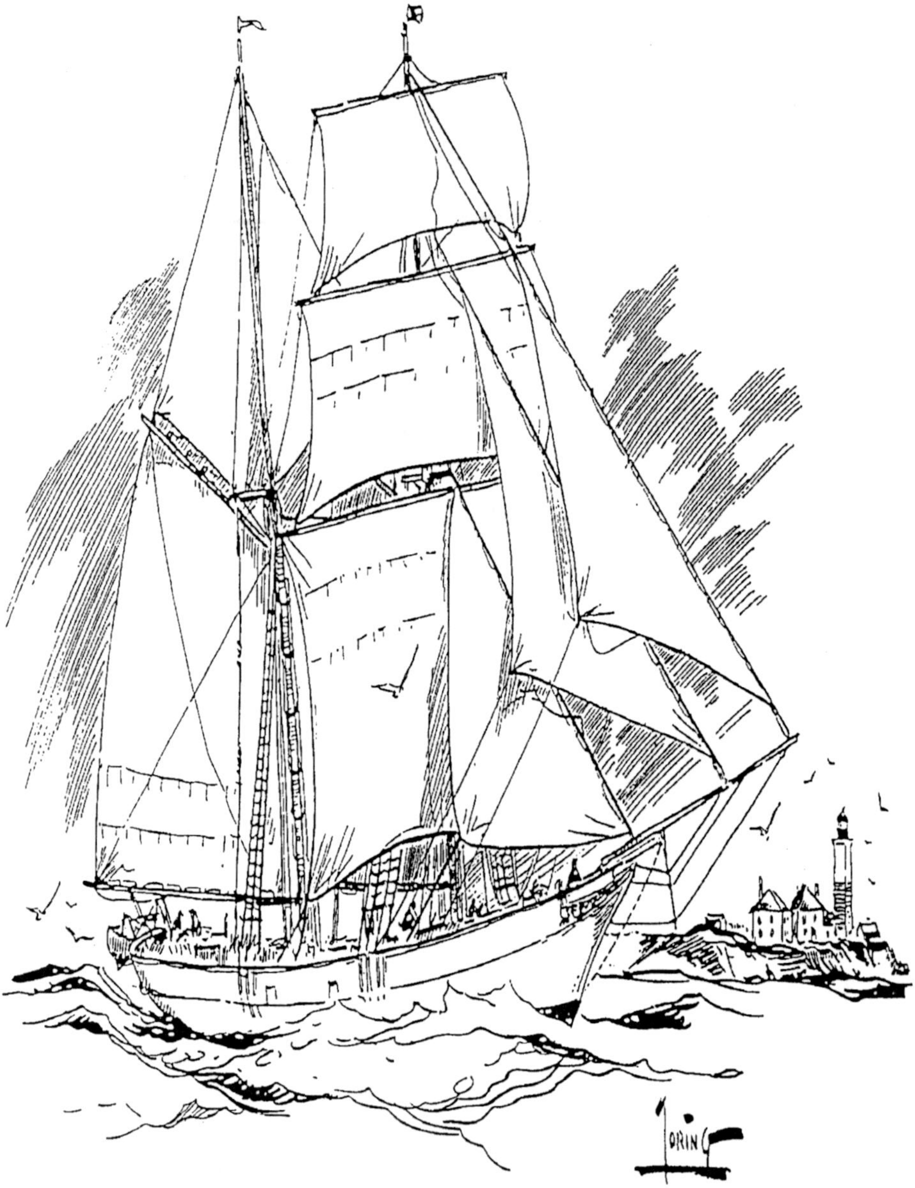

Table of Contents

FOREWORD	xv
DEDICATION	xvii
INTRODUCTION	xix
THE ILLUSTRATIONS	xxi
1. UTTERLY YANKEE	
Robert Frost	1
Mark Twain	2
"You Do The Same"	3
"That's a Lie"	4
"Far From Home"	4
"Remarks"	5
"Too Damn Cheap"	6
"The Town Sign"	7
"Store Bought Teeth"	7
"When It Does"	8
"Winter Vacation"	9
2. AROUND TOWN	
New England Dialects	11
Henry David Thoreau	13
"The Town Bum"	14
"Show & Tell"	15
"Five-Alarm Chili"	16
"Goodnight, Martha"	17
"Not Yours"	18
"Raising a Fire"	19
"The Intelligent Man"	19
"The Witness"	20
"Admit It"	21
"The New Privy"	21
"The Lantern"	22

3. YANKEE THRIFT
Publick Bills of Credit 25
Carlo "Charles" Ponzi 26
"Tripe" 28
"Ass Sets" 29
"The Bag Ain't Full" 30
"The Three Penny Tip" 31
"Hot Air" 32
"Just Barely" 32
"Matt's Bank Loan" 33
"Josiah's Business Trip" 34

4. THE COUNTRY STORE
The Yankee Tin Peddler 35
Calvin Coolidge 37
"The She-Bear" 38
"Your Dog Bite?" 39
"The German Visitor" 40
"What's That Noise?" 40
"She Scatters" 41
"Josiah's Skunk" 42
"The Thanksgiving Turkey" 43
"Fish Chowder" 43

5. THE CHURCH
The Pilgrims and the Puritans 45
Brook Farm and the Shakers 46
"You Broke My Cookies" 46
"The Man Couldn't Swim" 47
"Not According To Scripture" 48
"Uncut Homily" 48
"Jesus Shoes" 49
"The Whole Damn Load" 50
"Two Or Three Steps" 51

"Taking Up Music" 51
"Hand It To Him Myself" 52
"Not Today, Thank You" 53
"The Quahaug Quartet" 53

6. GRAVE HUMOR
Cemetery Stones 55
Lizzie Borden 56
"Up To the Cemetery" 57
"Gettin' Old" 58
"Ol' Hattie" 58
"Aunt Emma's Funeral" 59
"Kinda Peekid" 60
"Up She Comes!" 60
"The Body In the River" 61
"At the Burying Ground" 62
"Fresh As a Haddock" 63

BERT & I 65

7. PATENT MEDICINE
Old Time Remedies 67
Mary Baker Eddy 68
"The Party Line" 69
"Enoch's Heart Attack" 70
"Lose My Suction" 71
"A Pretty Good Job" 71
"President Harding" 72
"The Dirtiest Foot" 73
"My Convenience" 73
"The Bald Head" 74
"Enoch's Phone Call" 75
"Castor Oil" 75
"Cabin Fever" 76

8. POLITICS & PRIMARIES
The Blue Laws 77
Fred Tuttle 78
"He Won't Say" 79
"Not Even For Fun" 79
"She Ain't Decided" 80
"I Would Have Been a Democrat" 81
"Still a New Englander" 81

9. THE STATE STORE
State Stores and Package Stores 83
Joseph P. Kennedy, Sr. 83
"Visiting Grandfather" 84
"The Toilet Key" 85
"Barbados Rum" 86
"Judgment Day" 87
"The Beer Samples" 88
"Three Kinds of Turd" 89

10. HORSES & HORSELESS CARRIAGES
Concord Coaches 91
Tin Lizzies 91
"Dead Air Pocket" 92
"Don't Give a Damn" 93
"Which Way To Rumford Falls?" 93
"Tall Tale" 94
"Tourists" 95
"Horse Startin'" 96
"Kick Startin'" 97
"Whoa!" 98
"The Richfield Sign" 98
"Don't Look Too Good" 99
"One Sick Hog" 99
"That's Once" 100
"In The Bushes" 101

"Wives" 102
"Horse Trading" 102
11. NOR'EASTERS & SOU'WESTERS
The L Street Brownies 105
The World's Record Wind 106
"Mud Time" 107
"Get Any Frost?" 107
"Leakin' Roof" 109
"Don't Even Know It" 110
"You Stuck?" 110
"The Town Line" 111
"More Bull" 112
12. THE HUB OF THE UNIVERSE
Oliver Wendel Holmes, Sr. 113
Hasty Pudding & Harvard Lampoon 113
"A Visit To the City" 114
"Get Scrod" 115
"The Holdup" 116
"A Buck a Game" 116
"The Prodigal Son" 117
YANKEE DOODLE 119
13. NAUGHTY STORIES
Banned In Boston 121
The Old Howard and the Combat Zone 121
"A Whole New Crowd" 122
"What's It This Time, Junior?" 123
"Go Fly a Kite" 124
"Nice Day For It" 124
"The Surprise Party" 125
"Got the Grippe" 126
"In the Hay Loft" 126

14. THE COUNTY FAIR
The Cardiff Giant 129
The Great Danbury Fair 130
"Democrat Pies" 130
"The Barnstormer" 131
"Pig To the Fair" 132
"Matt's Racing Cow" 133
"The Purple Balloon" 135
"The Aeroplane Ride" 135
"Post Time" 136
"Right or Left" 137

15. GONE HUNTIN'
Champ of the Lake 139
Leon Leonwood Bean 140
"Henry's Hunting Trip" 141
"The Breakfast Sausages" 141
"Brake For Moose" 142
"The Pot Luck Beans" 143
"Hunting Bear" 143
"Shot For Grouse" 144
"The Big Catch" 145
"The Tremendous Ol' Bear" 146

16. THE FARM
The Farmers Almanac 147
Popular Songs 147
"I Had a Car Like That" 149
"Bull Powder" 149
"Matt's Dry Well" 150
"Three Dollars Enough?" 151
"There's More To Life" 152
"Stonewalls" 152
"Stud Service" 153

"The Time of Day" 154
"The Center of Things" 154
"Back From College" 155
"More Bull Troubles" 158
"The Dog Died" 158
"Too Much Arguing" 159
"The Little Turkey" 160
"Bull Shooting" 161
"Wore It Off" 161

17. WOODEN SHIPS & IRON MEN
Fool's Rules Regatta 163
The War of Long Island Sound 163
"The New Punt" 164
"Set Her Again" 165
"All I Know" 167
"They're Crawling!" 168
"Don't Want To Be Beholden" 168
"The Old Pilot Book" 169
"Hardly Got My Bait Back" 171
"Walt On the Train" 172
"The Headlands Have Sunk" 172
"Matt's Baby" 174
"Warm Water" 174
INDEX 175

xiv *New England Tall Tales & White Lies*

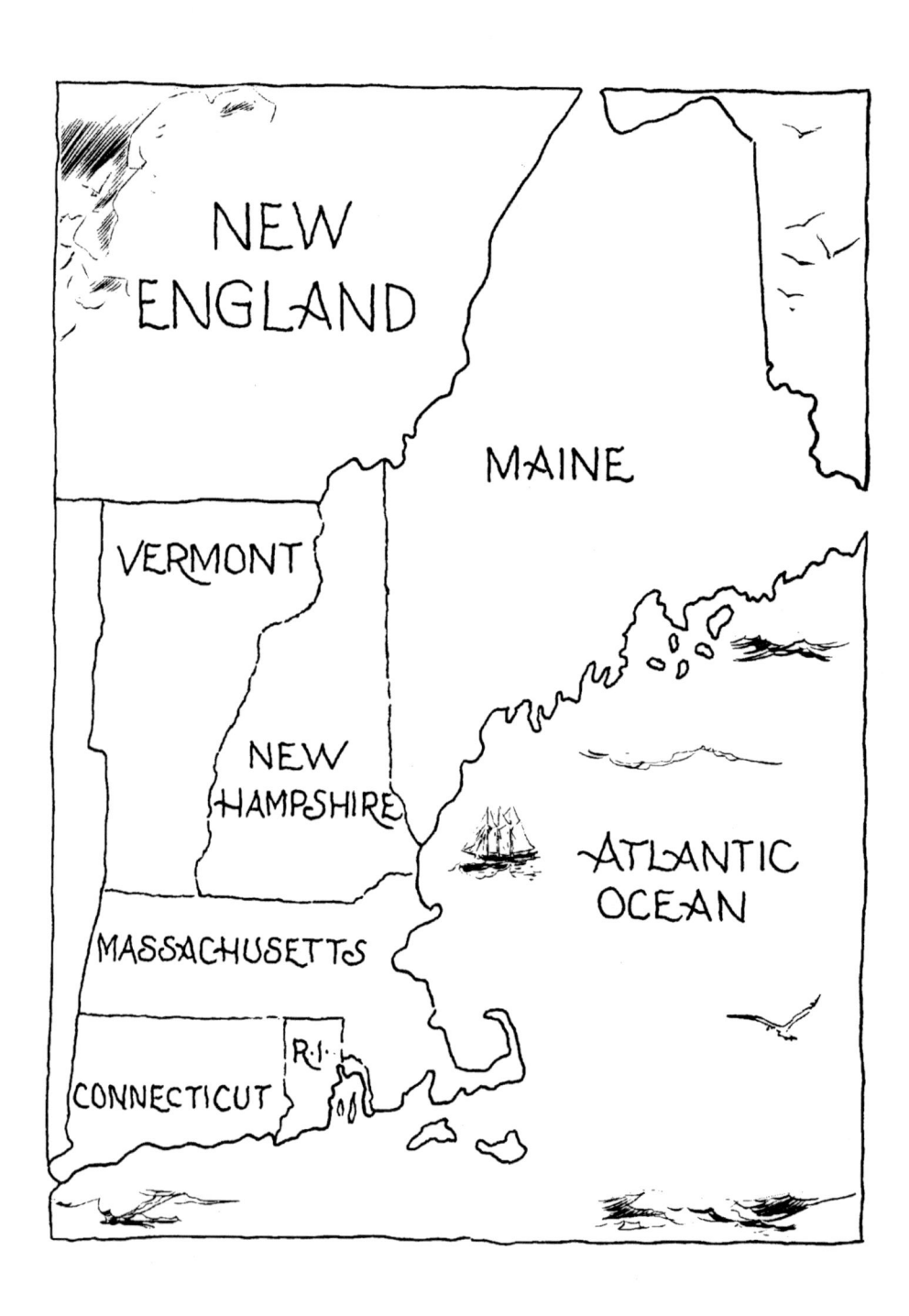

Foreword

I RECALL AS A YOUNG FELLAH hanging around Pitcher's Garage in Perryville, Rhode Island at coffee break time when all work paused and Stuart, the owner of the place with his brother Dave, would unwind a tale or two. It'd usually start with truth like the time he found a large snapping turtle down the bog behind the place. As Stuart recalled the situation, though, the creature and the yarn kept growing — so much so that by story's end Stuart had a beast so humungous, he had to haul it out with the wrecker.

Tall tales and yarns have been told at New England kitchen tables and around the potbelly stoves of country stores since forever. This Yankee humor, so called, are stories featuring dry wit often followed by a wry comeback or realistic recognition of a situation which, as Vermont storyteller Alan Foley once commented, "sits you on your ass."

Yankee humor is when a motorist asks a New Englander by the fork in the road, "Does it matter which way I take to White River Junction?" and he answers in all earnestness, "Not to me it don't."

Or the old-timer sitting on the country store steps when asked by a tourist, "You live here all your life?" replies in sincerity, "Not yet."

Many of the great old Yankee storytellers are gone now, but some of them had the good notion to record these tales on phonograph discs, and it is from these half-century old recordings that much of this material has been gathered. Also, some of these stories appear in slightly different tellings in my *New England Country Store Cookbook*. I mention this not because anybody gives a damn, but because I'm hoping to sell the cookbook.

Similar stories are frequently told by different fellahs in different ways, so some of these stories are edited compilations of various ideas. Among the Yankee storytellers represented in these pages are:

George Allen, Homer Babbidge, Stanley Foss Bartlett, Alan Bemis, Robert Bryan, John Cochran, Francis Colburn, Holman Day, Marshall Dodge, Allen Foley, Peter Gammons, James Garvin, Stevie Graham, Walter Hard, Frank Hatch, Lawrence Kilham, Peter Killham, Walter Kilham, William Lippincott, Kendall Morse, Bill Nye, Joe Perham, Tim Samples, Horace Stevens, Donald Tirrell, Artimus Ward, and many others to one degree or t'other.

Also, I offer my thanks to David Maslyn of the University of Rhode Island Special Collections unit and to Virginia Loring and Ron Loring for their help and remembrances.

Most of the stories are funny, family reading, but there are a few that must have originated over beer in the garage part of what were once called "filling stations", a place where calendar photographs of "pin-up" models were displayed, and where the fair sex wasn't enticed to tread.

— P.W.S.

*To Eddie Paul,
my son, friend, and a God-given gift,
who brings much humor to my life.*

xviii

Introduction

YANKEE HUMOR IS STORYTELLING by real people about other real people in situations that are generally exaggerated or completely made up. They are snapshots of a long ago time, when life was arduous but in retrospect seems simpler, uncluttered by affluence and superficiality. Everything counted. Life was authentic.

In order to preserve the bucolic lineage and era of these stories, we've created a cast of characters living in rural New England communities during the first half of the twentieth century:

The inland stories are placed in and around the fictional valley town of Center Northwood or in an imaginary river town beyond Granite Mountain called Rumford Falls. The coastal stories are set in Snug Harbour, an invented place whose designation reflects the British spelling, as do many actual New England place names.

The characters are introduced as neighbors through unfolding incidents in a lineal fashion, so it's advisable to read the stories from beginning to end as with any fictional narrative. Or at least until you get to know your neighbors.

Some of the language used here is archaic, slang, or just plain New England. For instance *tonic* — anyplace else the word is soda, but in eastern Massachusetts it's tonic, originating with naturally-brewed tonics such as root beer and sarsaparilla. *Collywobbles* is an archaic term for stomach upset — adult colic, so to speak. *Liz* is short for *tin Lizzie*, the nickname of Ford's Model T motorcar. And we'll encounter various old terms for farm implements, maritime equipment, and the other stuff of life that's explained as needed.

Now, to put yourself in a proper frame of mind: President Warren G. Harding has recently died in office, and his Vice President, Calvin Coolidge of Vermont, is now president. World War I ended a half decade ago.

By now New England, as with the rest of America, is emerging from the age of the horse into the age of horsepower, and half the motor vehicles on the roads are Ford Model T cars and trucks. At sea, sailing vessels are quickly giving way to motorcraft. Home entertainment is of the homemade variety — radio is just in its infancy and storytelling is fashionable. Popular music is distributed on Victrola records and on sheet music to be played in the parlor or in community halls. And "fellahs" is the over-used slang for men, "guys" not yet having imposed itself into the vernacular.

And the stories recalled here are authentic and traditional except where literary license is shamelessly employed.

The Illustrations

Wickford Harbor and Loring's Shanty

WHEREAS THE STORIES IN THIS BOOK originated in New England during the first half of the twentieth century, it seems appropriate that the accompanying illustrations are also born of that place and time. Drawn by the renowned New England illustrator Paule Loring, these pen sketches are simple reflections of these simpler times, each with the reverence or humor warranted.

Paule Loring, whose life began in Portland, Maine at the start of the twentieth century, moved in 1937 with his wife, Virginia, to Wickford, Rhode Island where he created most of his work at a dockside studio called Loring's Shanty. A prolific artist known for his speed in drawing, Paule abundantly illustrated the New England of his era for various publications including *Yachting, Skipper, Popular Boating, This Week,* and *Maine Coast Fisherman.*

Paule also served as political cartoonist for *The Providence Journal*, becoming notorious for submitting cartoons with a drawing on the envelope — often with the envelope being funnier than the cartoon inside.

His books include *Three Sides To the Sea, Never Argue With the Tape, This Really Happened In Rhode Island, Wickford Memories*, and with Virginia *Lancelot the Swordfish, Paule Loring's Marine Sketchbook*, and *Dud Sinker, Lobsterman*.

Something of a local character, Paule often sailed the New England waters in his Block Island double-ender schooner, GLORY ANNA II, once heading out in pea soup fog to greet the MAYFLOWER II on her first visit to Narragansett Bay.

On another occasion Paule set off overboard to cut a line entangled around the propeller and learned the hard way that the rudder notch wasn't merely decorative but the only way back aboard.

Paule died in 1968 at age sixty-eight, and his beloved schooner now berths in the permanent collection of the Mystic Seaport nautical museum in Connecticut.

1.
Utterly Yankee

TO UNDERSTAND THE CHARACTER OF YANKEE HUMOR is to understand the nature of old-line New Englanders, which can be described as independent, emotionally reserved, and thrifty. Robert Frost captures the Yankee spirit in his "The Road Not Taken", a poem describing a man standing at a rural junction in autumn:

> *Two roads diverged in a wood, and I —*
> *I took the one less traveled by,*
> *And that has made all the difference.*

The restrained nature of the Yankee can be modeled as: "If you really want to go, we'll go" being a show of enthusiasm; or "Well, that's good" being a sign of extraordinary praise. A New Englander isn't given to demonstrative behavior, but this seeming chill is merely a façade hiding unquestioned loyalty, respect, soundness of spirit, and a wink of the eye. All of which are the fruits of a deep-rooted heritage and genealogy. Yankees have a strong sense of where they are going based on where their ancestors have been, so perhaps it's this confidence which breeds an assuredness experienced among few other Americans.

In New England, friendship is bond, and to understand this is to grasp this little story about Robert Frost who, although the consummate Yankee, was born in San Francisco.

Mr. Frost was visiting Thomas Reed Powell, the distinguished professor at Harvard Law School who is remembered for writing among other things, "If you think that you can think about a thing inextricably attached to something else without thinking about the thing it is attached to, then you have a legal mind."

In the course of a vehement discussion, Mr. Powell, quick to recall Mr. Frost's pedigree says, "You, Frost, are merely a bastard Yankee," to which Mr. Frost equally abrupt replies, "Yes, and you, Powell, are merely a Yankee bastard." With New Englanders it's sometimes difficult to discern whether they're friends or antagonists.

☞ Samuel Langhorne Clemens, "Mark Twain", discovered the restrained nature of the Yankee first hand. Many people perhaps assume Mr. Twain wrote his stories while piloting sternwheelers along the Mississippi River, but in fact he wrote *The Adventures of Tom Sawyer*, *The Adventures of Huckleberry Finn*, and other novels not far from the banks of the Connecticut River at his home on Farmington Avenue in Hartford.

The Mark Twain House is a nineteen-room mansion that serves today as a National Landmark museum. Of his house Mr. Twain wrote, "We never came home from an absence that its face did not light up and speak out its eloquent welcome, and we could not enter unmoved."

During these years Mark Twain also toured, giving what was billed as A HUMOROUS LECTURE, a distasteful chore for Mr. Twain necessitated by his seemingly perpetual desire to invest in unproved inventions. One such lecture took him up the Connecticut River to the Opera House in Brattleborough, Vermont where he received the then-staggering fee of one hundred dollars — this in a day when his *A Connecticut Yankee in King Arthur's Court* was fetching a mere two dollars in the illustrated deluxe, English silk-bound edition.

In presenting his oration in Brattleborough one thing Mr. Twain hadn't anticipated was this characteristic Yankee reserve, so in delivering his lecture and not receiving the expected response, he became bothered enough to end his talk prematurely, left the stage to polite applause, and went around to the lobby to see what was wrong. Soon an elderly couple emerged, leaving to go home.

"Warn't he funny. Warn't he funny," Mr. Twain heard the old gentleman say, "Why, it was all I could do to keep from laughing."

You Do The Same

Up in Center Northwood, as is true of most of upcountry New England, there's a village emporium catering to all of the needs and most of the wants of the folks living here and about. That place is called Peterson's Country Store, and our friend, Bill Peterson, handles the business by himself since his wife died five years ago.

Bill's is a fairly typical country store in that it's crammed to the ceiling with everything from canned vegetables and magazines to flannel shirts and snow shovels. And it serves the community as the only shopping around with a product line worthy of towns anywhere.

In addition to stocking provisions and supplies, Bill also serves as notary public, postmaster, and agent for the Trailways bus company, whose bus comes by every Monday, Wednesday, and Friday.

Frank Perry is the bus driver, and on one Wednesday afternoon Frank pulls up in front as he does, gets out to use the outhouse behind the store, buys a Moxie soda, then checks to see if anybody showed up to ride.

He's just settling back into the driver's seat when Jeremiah Coates, Josiah's youngest, comes running up followed by his father's scruffy old dog. "Hey, fellah," Frank snaps, "You ain't bringing that mutt on my bus."

Well, that sets Jeremiah off something wicked, and he starts into a verbal rampage that — well, let's just say you wouldn't want your dear old grandmother to hear such talk. He rants and raves then finally screams, "You sonuvabitch, you know what you can do with your damn bus!"

"Listen, fellah," Frank shouts back, "If you do the same with that dog, you can get on."

That's A Lie

In upcountry New England a narrow pass between mountains is called a *notch*, and if you take Old Notch Road from Center Northwood down between Granite Mountain and Sugar Hill, you'll eventually come to the traffic circle at the Coast Road. A little further past that on an old gravel road is Salt Cove and the fishing village of Snug Harbour.

Harry Babcock and his wife, Mary, are the proprietors of the Whaler's Inn over there, and one morning Harry's down to the front desk, when a woman lumbers toward him looking not one bit pleased.

"Mr. Babcock," she proclaims.

"What's your problem?" asks Harry.

"I have a complaint," she says.

"Very well," replies Harry, "What's the complaint?"

"One of your waitresses just spilled cream on my brand new dress," the woman grumbles.

"That's a lie from the start," says Harry, "I happen to know there's not a drop of cream in the house."

Far From Home

On the way along Old Notch Road is Cloverdale Farm, and old Enoch Webster raises Holsteins and Ayrshires up there. He'd considered getting Jerseys, but you know what they say about Jersey owners: they're too poor to raise a cow and too proud to own a goat.

Enoch recently turned ninety-six, but he's really not a natural citizen. He was actually born out west in New York state, and never even set foot in these parts until he was three years old. Nevertheless, he goes on letting folks think he's from around here.

At some point every year or so Enoch takes the Trailways bus down to South Station in Boston, catches a train, and visits an old buddy from his Army regiment now living down the Lone Star state.

On one such tour down Texas, Enoch spots what to him is the most peculiar of sights — astonishing plants with long orange flowers sticking right out of them.

"What's that damn thing?" Enoch inquires, taken aback.

"That, my friend, is a bird of paradise!" replies his buddy.

Well sir, New Englanders are enlightened enough to know the difference between a plant and a bird, and besides that, Yankees know that the drab Texas rangeland doesn't begin to compare to the lush, green meadows and mountains of New England — which is apparently clear to most everybody save Texans.

"Bird of paradise?" Enoch snorts, "It's it a mite far from home, ain't it?"

Remarks

Up here in the slanted hill country of New England we have barns you can walk into on the front side, but that drop off two or three stories on the back. And that's just the way it is at Fairview Farm down there off the Coast Road where the land makes a quick dash to the shore.

Seth Thayer, who owns the place, is up on his barn roof replacing shingles blown off during that last nor'easter when he loses his footing, falls off the steep side, and dies. The day of the funeral his son, Nate, comes down from the Center to Charley Snow's funeral parlor with his family, then after the funeral he heads over to the insurance agent's to fill out some forms.

"On what date was the accident?" the agent inquires.

"Last Tuesday afternoon," Nate replies.

"Where did the accident occur?" the agent wants to know.

"On his farm," says Nate.

"What was the nature of the injuries?" the agent asks.

"Gawd, he busted his neck," Nate tells him, and so it went until the agent concludes.

"That's it for my formal questions," the agent tells him, "Are there any final remarks?"

"I don't believe he made none," replies Nate.

Too Damn Cheap

Well sir, young Jeremiah Coates finally got down to Boston for Gawd knows what iniquity, and he's now on the bus returning home. As he sits watching the countryside roll by, he happens to glance across the aisle and notices Horace Peckham with a watch chain dangling from his belt, reading *The Boston Post*.

"You mind telling me the time of day?" Jeremiah asks.

"Nope," says Horace, hardly looking up.

"You've got a watch chain there," Jeremiah persists, "Why won't you tell me what time it is?"

Horace is sort of perturbed by the interruption as he looks up again.

"Listen, son," he says, "If you insist on pestering me like this, I'll tell you. If I were to tell you the time of day, it wouldn't be too long before we got to talking about fishing. Next thing I'd tell you I enjoy fishing, and you'd tell me you like fishing, too. Now, since we're riding along some of the finest trout streams in New England, I'd admit I live on the best fishing spot on Arrow Lake.

"Next thing, I'll invite you to come to my house, and you'll accept. After supper we'll sit in my den drinking and talking about fishing. We might even go out and do a little fishing. Since it'd gotten late, I'll invite you to stay the night, and naturally you'll accept. During the night, given we'd been doing all that drinking, you'll have the necessity to get up. Since you're in a strange house, you'll stagger about in the dark some, and eventually you'll stumble into my daughter's room."

"Now, you're a mighty fine looking young fellah, so naturally, the next morning I'll have occasion to force you to marry my daughter, and to tell you the truth, I don't want no son-in-law whose too damn cheap to carry a watch."

The Town Sign

While he was down Texas visiting, Enoch Webster receives a letter from Margaret Andrews, the town clerk, informing him that the old family homestead up Granite Mountain had been set ablaze by some Northwood Academy boys who'd gone up there camping and to smoke cigarettes.

The old Webster homestead hasn't been used since Enoch's mother passed away some twenty years ago. Margaret's letter also mentions that the town put up a sign on the property. Since she doesn't indicate what the sign says, and he's a mite curious, Enoch writes back.

It takes a couple of weeks for Margaret's reply to arrive, and when it does Enoch opens it up and reads, "The sign you inquired about is shaped like an arrow and says 'Center Northwood 9 Miles.'"

Store Bought Teeth

Tom Lillibridge is a young fellah who earns his living as a fisherman in Snug Harbour. As he heads down the dock in the early morning hours, he spots his employer, Walt Palmer, captain of the fishing smack DAUNTLESS, climbing up out of the bilge.

"G'morning, Cappy," Tom shouts.

"Ayah, Tom," Walt replies as Tom comes into close range.

"Whatcha chewing on, some of them Chiclets?" Tom jokes. Chiclets, in case you don't know, are an old-fashion white square confection made from tree gum.

"Gawd no," says Walt, "My wife bought me this set of store-bought teeth, and I've been a-working 'em and a-working 'em, but 'tis all I can do to keep 'em from falling out of my head."

"Just needs some adjusting, I suppose," Tom comments.

"I'll tell you this, Tom," Walt replies, "If I bought me one of them meat grinders and screwed it onto my dining room table, I'd be a damsite better off."

When It Does

Eileen Peckham is the most boisterous woman anyone has ever heard, yet Horace, her husband, is just as different as she be t'other way. All day long you can hear her bellowing at him, their children, and anyone foolish enough to call up on the telephone. But Horace hides behind his newspaper and just takes it in.

One time Bill Peterson, who runs the country store up Center Northwood, asked him why he married her. "It was the only arrangement I could make that was satisfactory to her father," Horace explained.

One evening after supper as Horace sits in the parlor reading *The Northwood Independent,* Eileen starts up again.

"I work myself to the bone, you know!" she bellows from the kitchen.

"That so?" he says.

"Yet you set about here like you haven't a care in the world!" she screams.

"Yep," he replies.

"What d'ya think?" she yells, "That supper cooked itself?"

"Ayah," he says.

"You know, someday something's going to happen to one of us," Eileen hollers, "Then you'll feel different!"

"When it does," Horace replies, "I'm moving down Rumford Falls."

The Winter Vacation

Seems more and more folks are migrating south for mid-winter vacations — though I don't know anybody around here who'd actually done it. Harry and Mary Babcock, though, think it sounds like a good idea, and because right after New Year's is such a slow time down Snug Harbour, they decide to close Whaler's Inn and head south.

Upon their return, they're up to Bill Peterson's Country Store stocking up on provisions.

"I wouldn't do it again," Harry admits to Bill, who is packing their supplies into a Pearson's cracker box.

"It sounded like a good idea," Mary adds.

"We spent all January on Nantucket Island," Harry says, "and I don't believe it was worth the effort."

10 New England Tall Tales & White Lies

Moxie™, America's first mass-marketed soda, was founded in 1884 in Lowell, Massachusetts as a medicinal "nerve food". After the passage of the U. S. Pure Food & Drug Act, Moxie was marketed as a soft drink with the jingle "Just Make It Moxie For Mine." Moxie was President Calvin Coolidge's favorite beverage.

2.
Around Town

TO APPRECIATE YANKEE HUMOR STORIES, you need only to read them, but to *tell* New England yarns, you need to speak the native tongue, which is more difficult than you might think since there really isn't any single New England accent or speech pattern.

New England dialects spring primarily from the melting pot of settlers and reflect each region's unique verbal stew. The accent in Maine and Vermont, for instance, reflect the early English settlers. In New Hampshire along the Merrimac River into Massachusetts, and also the Blackstone River, Connecticut River, and other New England waterways the spoken language is influenced by later immigrants, who labored in textile mills, shoe factories, and other water-driven industries.

Whereas in parts of rural, agrarian Maine the speech resembles the drawn, old English of Shakespeare's time, in parts of central Rhode Island the speech has a nasal twang. Fellahs getting together at a bar for *bee-AHS* in Maine, gather for *BEE-iz* in Rhode Island.

In Boston there's the clenched-teeth *HAA-vuhd* sound of the so-called Brahmin and also the "aw" sound, as in *HAW-vuhd*, of the blue-collar neighborhoods. Kevin White, the former mayor of Beantown, used to express frustration by bellowing, *"Maw-tha a Gawd!"* which transliterated is "Mother of God!"

Add to this variation of accents local phrases, missing syllables, added syllables, missing R's, and added R's, and it's a wonder anyone from Boston can summer in Maine and get along.

So here at great linguistic risk is a decidedly abridged, regionally mixed glossary of New England pronunciations to add color and confusion to your enjoyment of Yankee humor stories:

ahnt — Your uncle's wife.
ayah — Yes in downeast Maine.
ba'kun — *Baking*, as in "Maw-tha can't come to the telephone right now; she's *ba'kun* a py-he."
bang — As in "Bang a left at the next stop sign."
b'day-duhs — *Potatoes* in eastern Massachusetts.
bubbla — A drinking fountain.
can't-get — A negative-positive as in "Let's g'down en see if we can't-get cha'kah fixed."
cell-ah — The foundation of your house. The basement.
CS — The department store run by Mr. Roebuck and his partner.
gah-bidge — Wet kitchen refuse as opposed to dry trash.
grine-dah — A submarine sandwich in an Italian torpedo roll.
huh'en — *Hunting* in the Western Lakes Region of Maine.
jeet? — *Did you eat?*
kah-keez — *Car keys*.
keg-gah — A large party with beer, usually down the beach or by the river where the cops won't caa'cha.
mow-ah — Not less.
na-ah — No, as in "*Na-ah*, no friggin' way, man!"
nA-bah — The family next doe-wah.
onna-conna — As in "Onna-conna I don't even know how to explain this word."
pack-ee — A store where packaged booze is sold.
poddy plattah — A plate of food served at a party. (A keg-gah doesn't usually have a poddy plattah, just bags of b'day-dah chips for munchies.)
side-by-each — How y'pahk y'kah in Franco-Anglo Woonsocket, Rhode Island.
so-doan-eye — Another negative-positive meaning "me too".
sup? — *What's up?*, as in "how y'doin'?"

taw-nick — *Tonic*, carbonated soda in eastern Massachusetts.
wee-id — Unusual as in "He didn't show up to the keg-gah las'night; isn't that *wee-id*?"
yee-ah — As in "Y'comin' t'tha New *Yee-ah* seeve poddy? If y'show, bring bee-iz or some b'day-duh chips."

☛ Henry David Thoreau, the essayist and poet, was the embodiment of the New England independent mindset. He was also a highly educated bum, spending a sizable part of his life dependent upon Ralph Waldo Emerson, the renowned poet and breeder of an independent philosophy called New England Transcendentalism. It was apparently this independent free thinking which was the bond for Mr. Emerson and his fourteen-years-younger freeloader.

Mr. Thoreau was born in Concord, Massachusetts, then after attending Harvard University he followed a spotted career which included teacher, land surveyor, handyman, and appropriately for a writer, working in his father's pencil factory. In 1849 Mr. Thoreau pub-lished his first book, *A Week On the Concord and Merrimac Rivers*, which sold so poorly he commented, "I now have a library of nearly nine hundred volumes, seven hundred of which I wrote myself."

At the age of twenty-eight, Mr. Thoreau initiated one of his only successes when he took independence to its logical length and built his own shack, fending for himself on the shore of nearby Walden Pond. During these brief two years of tangible independence, Mr. Thoreau kept a journal that eventually became the basis of his *Walden, or Life In the Woods*, which describes his bean field, the pond in winter, and other philosophical stuff.

Although the book didn't sell like hot cakes at the time, Mr. Thoreau was characteristically philosophical. "I am grateful for what I am and have," he wrote, "My thanksgiving is perpetual. It is surprising how contented one can be with nothing definite; only a sense of existence." Then he went back to sponging off Mr. Emerson and his parents.

His essay, "Resistance to Civil Government", was the result of the perpetually broke Mr. Thoreau spending time in the Concord jail for not paying town taxes — allegedly as a protest against the Mexican War and slavery. After this term of sponging off the town ended, his essay was published as *Civil Disobedience,* and a century later would influence the nonviolent protests of Mahatma Gandhi against English imperialism in India and the positive resistance campaign of the Reverend Dr. Martin Luther King, Jr. against racial bias in the southern United States.

The Town Bum

Josiah Coates probably wasn't the kind of individualist Mr. Thoreau was philosophizing about, but I bet there's a fellah in most every town who has his own peculiar way of doing things. Josiah lives up Granite Mountain in an old trailer with a woodstove he fashioned from a rusty grease drum he'd found out back of Fred Johnson's Richfield filling station and garage. Not that he burns much wood in it.

Josiah's wicked lazy, so much so that despite the fact his trailer sets amid a woodlot, he's generally too lazy to go out and cut firewood. In those times when it's cold enough that steam rises from his sheets as it does from a manure heap, he goes out, fetches chunks of fallen tree limbs, and burns those.

Not to suggest Josiah's lazy in all things: over the years he's fathered a dozen or more offspring by other fellah's wives. Once at census time, an enumerator girl came by Josiah's trailer.

"How many children do you have, Mr. Coates?" she inquires.

"A few but only three I know about," Josiah replies, "Two living and one down Boston."

"Living alone this far from town as you do," she asks, "How'd you end up with so many children?"

"I got a bicycle," he tells her.

And Josiah used to be seen around Center Northwood riding his bicycle. One time when he rode over to Bill Peterson's Country Store, he was accompanied by an old dog he was too lazy to name and just called "Dawg".

"Where'd he come from?" Bill asks when they stroll in that first time.

"He just come up and licked my hand," Josiah tells him.

"Ever think of eating with a fork?" Bill asks.

Well sir, time passes with Josiah and Dawg becoming sort of a fixture down the Center. That is, until that day when Josiah comes around, and he's all by himself.

"Where's Dawg today?" Bill inquires.

"Oh Gawd, I had to shoot him," Josiah says.

"Was he mad?" Bill asks.

"I s'pose he warn't too damned pleased," Josiah replies.

And then there's his word. Let's just say Josiah's been known to take liberties with the truth. For instance, Josiah has some cows he lets roam around in that meadow up there, but he's such a liar that when it comes milking time, he has to get one of his sons to call them in.

"The worst lickin' I ever got," Josiah once admitted, "was for telling the truth."

"I must say it cured you," Bill told him.

Show & Tell

Horace and Eileen Peckham have a daughter, Harriet, who attends first grade up to Arrow Lake Grammar School. Thursday afternoon she came home from class with some exciting news.

"I sure caused a to-do in school today!" she proclaims to Eileen, who's boiling up a batch of rose hips jelly in her kitchen.

"How in the world did you manage to do that?" Eileen wants to know.

"Well, it was show and tell today, and Freddy Potter brought in his pet mouse", Harriet reports, "As we were passing it around the room, the mouse jumps out of my hands."

"And that scared teacher?" Eileen asks.

"I don't know about that," Harriet replies, "but when it ran up her leg, she jumped up, and you wouldn't believe the amount of water she squeezed out of that mouse."

Five-Alarm Chili

Lew Cottrell's Minuteman Diner sets down there at the traffic circle where Old Notch Road meets the Coast Road. One noontime a tourist couple comes in, settles into one of the polished hardwood booths, and looks over the menu, which is just a mimeographed sheet of paper in a plastic sleeve. After a spell, they settle on Lou's famous Five Alarm Chili.

Ann Champlin is the waitress over there, so she takes their order, and in a jiffy she delivers them two steaming bowls along with a couple of heavy white mugs of coffee and a basket of oyster crackers.

"Here you go," Ann says, setting the two porcelain bowls on the table. The fellah cautiously takes in a spoonful.

"Not very spicy," he comments. Then his wife takes in a bite.

"I don't suppose you have some chili powder or hot sauce in the kitchen, do you?" she inquires.

"No, we don't have any of that," Ann replies, "but we've got salt and pepper on the table, and I can fetch some ketchup, if you want."

Goodnight, Martha

Roger and Martha Hancock own Sugar Hill Farm and live there with their two boys, Joe and Kenny. They just had their twenty-fifth wedding anniversary and quite an affair it was! The ladies up to the Congregational Meeting House put it on, and did up the parsonage pretty much the way they'd thrown the wedding reception years ago.

Back then, Roger had kind of traipsed about a number of years, eventually finding Martha and getting around to marrying her. They had a nice ceremony up to the church, as I say, and Roger and Martha are feeling kinda puffed up and happy as they head up to his farm afterwards.

Martha is kind of nervous, not having been with a man before, but Roger, you know, he was kind of a "man about town", you might call it.

"There's one or two things I want you should know about me," he tells Martha, after they'd gotten settled into the farmhouse. "First of all, I get up at a quarter to six every morning, and I like to have my breakfast at six-fifteen. Now, I don't mean six o'clock, Martha, nor do I mean six-thirty, either. I take my breakfast at six-fifteen.

"Then I go out to do my chores, and I like to take my dinner at twelve o'clock noon. Now, I don't mean eleven forty-five, and I don't mean twelve-fifteen. I want my dinner at twelve o'clock punctual.

"As far as supper goes, I have my supper at five-thirty. If you call me at a quarter past five, I ain't a-going to be ready, and I don't mean five forty-five either. I want my supper at five-thirty.

"Now as far as taking my pleasure goes, I take my pleasure on Monday and Friday night. This is Saturday, goodnight Martha."

Not Yours

Each season many New England communities celebrate the bounties of nature with spring sugaring-off parties, summer seafood festivals, autumn harvest fairs, and winter ice-fishing derbies.

Oftentimes, too, pancake breakfasts, arts and crafts displays, merchandise exhibits, and other amusements accompany these festivities — as a matter of fact Ann Champlin, the waitress down to the Minuteman Diner, has an arts and crafts booth each summer at the Snug Harbour Lobster Festival.

It's a busy Friday night at the festival and there's a clambake being served in one tent, the children are riding the merry-go-round and Ferris wheel set up at the back of the gravel lot, and Tom Lillibridge, Matt Conley, and Joe Hancock, local boys, are performing sea chanteys on the stage, which is actually a couple of old dragger doors set upon some wooden soda crates borrowed from the refreshment stand.

The large exhibit tent is crowded, dusty, and loud when young Jeremiah Coates and Joshua Peckham descend upon Ann's little booth, pawing over her merchandise and upsetting her display. Ann endures this for longer than she feels necessary.

"Get lost you lousy brats!" she finally hollers at them. Well sir, Eileen Peckham, who you know can holler pretty good herself, is standing close enough to hear this.

"What's your difficulty, lady?" Eileen yells.

"These your brats?" Ann snaps back.

"Don't go calling my boy a brat," Eileen shouts, "Don't you like children?"

"Not yours," Ann replies.

Raising a Fire

Just before he married Lulu, Junior Coates decided to build them a cabin up Granite Mountain. After he got the walls and most of the roof up, Junior builds in a fieldstone fireplace off to one end of the room — though Junior being Junior, he naturally forgets to put in a damper. What he does remember is to provide for plenty of hot water by attaching one of those old-fashion cranes to the fireplace wall and hanging a twenty-gallon, cast iron kettle over where the fire will be.

Junior borrowed Larry, that ancient draft horse of his old man's, and dragged back a wide slab of flint rock for the hearth. Once the fireplace was finished, Junior then gathers some pine for kindling, cuts some oak logs, and lays them into the fireplace for the following morning.

Summer or winter, Junior never bothers to wear shoes, so the bottoms of his feet have become tough like boot leather. Come daybreak after he gets up, Junior goes over to his fireplace, scuffs his feet on the flint to raise sparks, and in no time kicks up a blaze.

Well sir, Junior does this every morning just the same way until that time an overnight cloudburst pours rain down his chimney and soaks his firewood. Next morning Junior gets up as usual and begins scuffing, but nothing happens. So he tries again, scuffing and scuffing, sparks are flying every which way — he even gets the water boiling and damn near burns down the cabin — but Junior never does get that fire started.

The Intelligent Man

Martha Hancock, Roger's wife, works part-time at the Ralph Waldo Emerson Public Library up the Center, checking out books and maintaining a hush worthy of a Trappist monk.

She's working at the circulation desk in the Central Reading Room one morning when she hears a murmur from behind a bookshelf. Supposing it to be students from Northwood Academy across the athletic field behind the library, she sneaks with cat-like stealth around the bookshelf, where she discovers Henry Foster sitting there by himself reading a *National Geographic*.

"You haven't seen any youngsters back here?" she asks.

"No one but me," Henry smiles.

Martha returns to the desk when she hears the murmuring again. Perplexed, she goes back to find Henry still reading just as before. Being careful not to disturb him, Martha quietly withdraws back to the desk, when she once again hears the murmur.

Now she's certain someone is playing a prank, purposely causing commotion to no purpose save a juvenile escapade. So this time Martha stealthily circles the perimeter of the reading room intent on revealing the scoundrel and exposing his strident deed. But as she silently glides around from the back of the room, she once again comes upon Henry, alone reading aloud to himself.

"Oh, it's you I heard!" she says with surprise.

"Ayah, just me," says Henry, "Sometimes I just like talking to an intelligent man, and what's more I enjoy hearing an intelligent man speak."

The Witness

A fight broke out in Center Northwood and Enoch Webster just happened to witness it. So when the case came up in Judge Pratt's courtroom, Enoch is called in to testify.

"How far were you from the altercation, Mr. Webster?" the lawyer asks.

"Ten feet, four and three quarter inches," Enoch tells him.

"How'd you know that so precisely?" the lawyer wants to know.
"Because I measured it," Enoch says.
"Why in the world would you do that?" the lawyer inquires.
"Because I knew some damn fool would ask," Enoch replies, "and you did."

Admit It

In the old days, many of the upcountry high schools were known as "academies" — even today many still are. Josiah Coates has been called down to Northwood Academy. Once again there's a discipline problem with his youngest son, Jeremiah.

It seems Jeremiah's class was taking a history test, and after the question, "Who wrote the Declaration of Independence?" he answered, "Damned if I know."

"What do you think we should do about this?" Mr. Johnson, the headmaster, asks Josiah, who's turning red with rage. He grabs Jeremiah by the shirt collar and starts yelling.

"If you're the one who wrote on that damn thing," Josiah hollers, "Then you just best admit it!"

The New Privy

Charley Snow runs the funeral parlor next door to his house, and he usually gets Walt Palmer to build his coffins. So, when Charley decided he needed a new outhouse, naturally he asks Walt to build it for him.

"Where you looking to put it?" Walt asks Charley as he gazes across the yard behind the house.

"Walt, I was thinking," Charley says, "Maybe down there by the lilacs might be good, and it will look mighty pretty come spring."

"It's your privy," says Walt.

So Walt starts working and had gotten the floorboards nailed in when Charley comes by.

"Walt, I've been thinking," says Charley. "If it's down there by the lilacs, it's going to be a mite far come winter, but if it's over here next to the balsams, it'll look pretty even in the cold months."

"It's your privy," says Walt.

After a spell while Walt's up on the roof nailing the shingles, Charley comes by again.

"Walt, I've been thinking," says Charley. Seems to me if it's over here by the balsams, what with the prevailing winds sou'west and the house nor'east, it would be a mite uncomfortable for the missus in the kitchen come summer. But if it's half way between the balsams and the lilacs, then it wouldn't be too far come winter, nor too close come summer."

"It's your privy," says Walt.

Walt's finishing the interior and is about to nail in the boxwood seat when Charley comes by again.

"Walt, I've been thinking," Charley says, "It might be better if you put in two holes instead of just the one."

"You sure?" Walt asks.

"Why?" Charley replies.

"Well, it's your privy, Charley," Walt says, "but sometime you'll need to come out here in a hurry, and by the time you make up your mind, it'll be too damn late."

The Lantern

Junior Coates is a lot like his father, Josiah, which is to say he's not the sharpest tack on the Lord's corkboard. And akin to his old man, Junior and his wife, Lulu, have squeezed out quite a load of children — though this last time was quite an event. Lulu started contractions in the middle of the night, which she'd never done before, so Junior gets the hot water, towels, and a lantern, then sits by and waits.

In nearly no time the baby pops out, and Junior springs into action, catching the child and cleaning up as he has on every other occasion. But no sooner as he's done, Lulu starts in once more, and Junior yet again springs to action, fetches more water and towels, catches the baby, and cleans up.

Junior's just about finished, when Lulu starts all over again. This time, though, Junior quickly turns and with a mighty puff, blows out that lantern.

"What'd ya do that for?" Lulu screams in the dark, along with the contractions.

"It's the light!" Junior snaps, "It's attracting them."

Snug Harbour on an overcast day.

3.
Yankee Thrift

NEW ENGLANDERS ARE NATURALLY THRIFTY, conservative in all matters of money and finance, the prevailing attitude being "make do or do without, eat it up or can it." Although it's difficult to point to any single occurrence that may have led to such monetary caution, without doubt one contributing factor was the currency mess during colonial times.

New-England, as the region was known back then, comprised the governments of Massachusetts Bay (which included the land area of Maine), New-Hampshire, Rhode-Island, and Connecticut. Vermont at that time was an independent republic — and still is in many respects.

In order for these governments to reimburse vendors and service providers, they issued Publick Bills of Credit, which would be redeemed at a "distant day" after supporting tax money had been raised. This was awkward, to say the least, but it worked in its own way, or at least it did until the soldiers returned from the Battle of Québec and needed to be paid.

As usual, Publick Bills of Credit were issued, but the fellahs needed the government to "pay the bill" now, not later. This delay of payment caused most of them to sell their bills at discounts of thirty to forty percent to speculators who held the bills until the supporting tax funds were levied — not unlike the paycheck cashing schemes of today.

Unfair as this was, this was how business was conducted until 1749 after the French and Indian War when soldiers once again returned from the battlefield to receive promissory notes from the government. One protest pamphlet of the time stated:

> **One would think, that with People making a high Profession of Religion, there should need no other argument to reconcile them to Act than...that Truth and Justice, after having been banish'd near forty-years, are in a fair Way to return again.**

This time, however, the British government had staked part of the war expense, so the Massachusetts Bay General Court ordered that all Publick Bills of Credit be redeemed in silver dollars, one dollar for each forty-five shillings "billed".

But that wasn't the end of it. Now came the fear that if merchants received silver, they'd use it in foreign trade and eventually there would be no silver left to back the currency. Long story short, the government continued to buy now and pay later, which it still does today.

☞ Another occurrence that may have led to fiscal caution on the part of New Englanders was an investment scheme devised by an infamous Boston swindler named Carlo "Charles" Ponzi.

In November 1903 at the age of twenty Mr. Ponzi emigrated from Italy to Boston and for the next fourteen years drifted from town to town living off odd jobs. Finally, back in Boston working as a clerk for an international firm, Mr. Ponzi learned something that would transform his fate.

International Postal Reply Coupons were vouchers purchased overseas then redeemed by the United States Post Office Department for postage stamps. What caught Mr. Ponzi's eye was that postal coupons purchased in Spain for the equivalent of one cent when redeemed in Boston were worth six one-cent stamps, so he tried turning over such coupons himself and quickly discovered that agent fees and shipping consumed most of his profits.

Since he'd initially supposed the scheme a good one, however, Mr. Ponzi presumed other people would also suppose it a good idea. So on December 26, 1919 Mr. Ponzi gave himself a Christmas present and established a new company, The Security Exchange Company. He pitched that he could double investors' money in ninety days, which he did, and soon the needy and the greedy beat a path to his door.

Thousands of people bought promissory notes from Mr. Ponzi, and he dutifully paid them off with cash from later investors. It was an old-fashioned pyramid scheme, of course, but soon his desk drawers were literally stuffed with other people's money — and he was living the rich life in his mansion in Lexington. By summer Mr. Ponzi and his newly hired staff were taking in a million dollars a week, so he began opening branches across New England.

As with Publick Bills of Credit generations earlier, promises and reality can be two different things. On July 26, 1920 *The Boston Post* questioned the legitimacy of Mr. Ponzi's claims. His books were audited, and on August 10 his company was declared bankrupt.

Mr. Ponzi was arrested *twice*, first by federal authorities then by the authorities of the Commonwealth of Massachusetts. The subsequent investigation revealed that although forty thousand people had invested fifteen million dollars — about one hundred forty million dollars in today's money — only *two* International Postal Reply Coupons had actually been purchased.

Mr. Ponzi was sentenced to five years in Federal Prison followed by another seven in Massachusetts then released on a fourteen thousand dollar bond. He fled a month later, got involved in a swamp land swindle in Florida, yet another scam in Texas, and was eventually arrested in New Orleans.

In a move of desperation and gall, Mr. Ponzi then telegraphed President Calvin Coolidge hinting of connections between them at the Massachusetts State House on Beacon Hill, where the president had previously served as governor:

> **WESTERN UNION TELEGRAM**
>
> HIS EXCELENCY CALVIN COOLIDGE
> PRESIDENT OF THE UNITED STATES
> WASHINGTON D C
>
> PERSONALLY KNOWING EVENTS DOINGS AND PERSONS ON BEACON HILL MAY I ASK YOUR EXCELLENCY FOR OFFICIAL OR UNOFFICIAL INTERVENTION IN MY BEHALF? THE PONZI CASE HAS ASSUMED THE PROPORTIONS OF A NATIONAL SCANDAL FOSTERED BY THE STATE OF MASSACHUSETTS WITH THE FORBEARANCE OF THE FEDERAL GOVERNMENT. I CANNOT SILENTLY SUBMIT TO FURTHER PERSECUTION BUT, FOR THE BEST INTEREST OF ALL CONCERNED, I AM WILLING TO SUBMIT TO IMMEDIATE DEPORTATION. WILL YOUR EXCELLENCY GIVE HIS CONSIDERATION OF THE EVENTUAL WISDOM OF MY COMPROMISE?
> CHARLES PONZI

The president ignored him, naturally, so the father of the "Ponzi Scheme" did his time, was released, then fled for Italy, eventually to work as a translator for the fascist dictator, Benito Mussolini.

Tripe

In case you don't know, tripe is the stomach lining of cattle and oxen and is very rarely used as food, at least not in New England. In fact, as cuisine it's so poor that the term "that's tripe" has come to mean something is worthless or offensive.

That said, Walt Palmer just might be the thriftiest fellah in Snug Harbour. Walt's so cautious with his money that when he takes his horse and wagon up Center Northwood, he wears a union suit his wife sewed a money pocket onto.

On one of those occasions when he was up the Center, Walt wanders into Bill Peterson's Country Store and strolls up to the meat case.

"What can I get you?" Bill inquires.

"Tripe," Walt says.

"Godfrey mighty, Walt," Bill says, "You sure your missus wouldn't rather have some of this nice pot roast?"

"Listen, Bill, I didn't come in here for oratory," Walt says, "Do you or don't you have tripe?"

"Hold your horses, Walt," Bill says, as he slowly saunters to the back room knowing he's not making any money on this transaction.

In a little while Bill returns with a package wrapped in white butcher paper with a green string tied around it and hands it to Walt.

"I'm not even going to charge you," Bill tells him, "seeing's I'd have chucked this into the renderings bucket anyway."

Since Walt's already done this once before down the Snug Harbour Grocery, he assumed it would be on the house, so he thanks Bill and starts for the door.

"I don't get it though," Bill says to him, "Up here folks don't generally eat their critters that close."

Ass Sets

Josiah Coates is, as they say, mighty small potatoes and few in the hill, but there's that time he dabbled in private enterprise. Not that he was any more honest then than he is now.

Too few folks around anymore remember the summer Josiah decided to go into the real estate business — though nobody could quite figure out why since nearly everyone in these parts either lives in the family homestead or on the family farm. It's almost certain he started this venture for no other reason than he'd seen a sign in the window of the Northwood Bank & Trust Company advertising an office for rent.

"We have to be careful to whom we rent this since this room sets right over our vault," Mr. Harvey, the bank manager, told him. Since Josiah is a wicked liar and not a bank robber, that seemed to meet the requirements.

What with the vault downstairs, this state of affairs gives Josiah what he considers a good idea. He rearranges the furniture in the office placing the desk and chairs directly over the vault, then the next morning Josiah nails up a sign that reads:

> JOSIAH COATES, REAL ESTATE AGENT
> ASS SETS OVER TWO MILLION DOLLARS

The Bag Ain't Full

As you know, the typical Yankee is exceptionally cautious in regards to finances, and particularly in regards to handling the common purse. As often happens in New England, the country storekeeper also serves as postmaster, and so it is here.

On one occasion, Bill Peterson is tending to a customer when a call comes in from the Post Office Department down Boston.

"I'd like to speak to your postmaster," the postal voice says.

"Yes?" Bill replies.

"This is the regional bureau," the voice continues, "and we've received a report that no mail has been shipped from your post office in over two weeks."

"Yep", Bill says.

"Is there something wrong?" the postal voice inquires.

"Nope," Bill tells him.

"So, why isn't the mail going out?" the voice asks.

"You need to realize this is a small town," Bill reminds him.

"We understand that," the postal voice replies, "but are you saying there hasn't been any mail posted in all this time?"

"Of course not," Bill says.

"Then why hasn't your mail been shipped out?" the voice demands to know.

"Be patient," Bill admonishes the postal voice, figuring this to be one more instance of government bureaucracy frittering away the public's money. "It's been a damn slow month, and the bag ain't full yet."

The Three Penny Tip

Sometimes there are occasions when you'd prefer to speak plainly, but the place or situation dictates you keep a civil tongue in your head. Not that calling somebody a "bastard" wouldn't be appropriate, just sometimes you need to express it in a courteous way:

So it was over the Minuteman Diner when Henry Foster comes in. He runs the coaster PILGRIM, a cargo schooner, and strongly believes the adage, "a penny saved is a penny earned." That being fact, this is a rare occasion Henry treating himself to a restaurant supper of hot dogs, beans, and brown bread.

After he'd cleared his plate as much as any man can and having paid the check, leaving behind a three-cent tip, Henry's just about to depart when Ann Champlin, the waitress, comes up.

"You know", she says, "I can tell a lot about a fellah just by the tip he leaves."

"That so?" says Henry.

"Yes I can," Ann says, "For instance this first penny indicates you are a thrifty man."

"Ayah, that's correct," Henry replies.

"And this second penny here tells me you're a bachelor," she tells him.

"Ayah, that's also correct," Henry says, "I admit, you amaze me."

"Thanks," Ann says as she turns to walk away.

"But what about this third penny," Henry wants to know, "What does that penny indicate?"

"That penny," says Ann, "tells me your father was a bachelor, too."

Hot Air

You recall that Josiah Coates had that so-called real estate office over the Northwood Bank & Trust Company. Well, an unsuspecting New York couple comes in one afternoon to inquire about the quality of life around here.

"I understand the air is more healthful," the lady states.

"Don't know but what 'tis," Josiah tells the couple, "As a matter of fact Enoch Webster went down Texas, took sick, and died. When the box arrived at Charley Snow's funeral parlor, he lifted the lid, and Enoch stood right up and walked home."

"Is that so?" the gentleman replies, "Seems to be quite a few folks in that burying ground by the church."

"That's another thing," Josiah tells them, "The selectmen had to hire a fellah from Boston to shoot hisself, just so they could start that cemetery."

Just Barely

Walt Palmer's always been money-wise, and for some months he has been storing his riches under his mattress. Now, however, his savings have lumped up and gotten uncomfortable, so Walt decides he best do something about this.

Last Wednesday there was a wicked gale, and since he couldn't put out for fishing, Walt decides to gather up his sizeable load of bills, leap into Old Liz, his Model T pickup truck, and trundle up to the Northwood Bank & Trust Company to turn them in.

Stepping up to the teller's cage, he dumps the whole mess right there onto the counter.

"If it won't trouble you," Walt says to the young fellah at the window, "I should like to exchange these bills for century notes."

The fellah gathers up the load, telling Walt that he has to take it over to the counting table to sort and bundle.

"You'll find seven hundred dollars there," Walt says, "Exactly."

After the teller had bundled the bills and returned to the window, he tells Walt there is, indeed, seven hundred total, and then counts out seven crisp one hundred dollar notes. Walt then takes them and in full view of everyone counts them again forwards then once again backwards.

"It's all there," the teller tells him somewhat defensively.

"That's correct," says Walt, "just barely."

Matt's Bank Loan

Matt Conley went into the Northwood Bank & Trust Company early last winter to get a business loan. He wanted to build a produce stand and souvenir shop on the Coast Road that the tourists use. Matt walks right in to talk to Mr. Harvey, the bank manager, who naturally has some questions about it.

"If I understand this entirely," he says to Matt, "you want to develop an enterprise on the Coast Road side of your farm."

"Yep," Matt says, "I guess you could call it that."

"And you are requesting a bank loan of three hundred dollars?" Mr. Harvey asks, "Is that right?"

"If you got that much," Matt says.

"Do you have any encumbrances on this property?" Mr. Harvey inquires.

"Not yet," Matt says, "but I'll be building one this spring."

Josiah's Business Trip

Some years back when Josiah Coates was trying to pass himself off as a real estate agent, he decides to take a business trip down Boston. Now, Josiah no more has business in Boston than he has business going to Boston, nevertheless since he'd never been on a train before, he wants to go.

Josiah, you know, isn't the most upright fellah around, and he usually smells like hen dressing. So when the conductor comes along wanting to collect his ticket and Josiah doesn't have one, the conductor takes a whiff of that bag of his and throws it off the platform into a puddle. Godfrey, that tees Josiah off.

"Not only do you try to fleece me," he hollers at the conductor, "but you damn near drown my little boy, Jeremiah."

4.
The Country Store

YANKEE HUMOR IS USUALLY SLICES OF LIFE that gently poke fun in sparing ways that are both obvious yet unexpected. Like when one fellah asks another, "How's your wife?" and gets the reply, "Compared to what?"

President Calvin Coolidge of Vermont, "Silent Cal", was famous for his economy with words. His wife, Grace, told of the time he was challenged by a dinner companion who bet she could get him to say three words. Mr. Coolidge turned to her and replied, "You lose."

Oftentimes this humor, these slices of life, are heard in rural country stores over unhurried games of checkers by the potbelly woodstove. Similarly in urban New England stories and yarns are heard in corner "spas" at the soda fountain counter over hefty white mugs of coffee *reg'lah* — some cream, two sugars. However, the initial exchange of these tales undoubtedly began not at the area gathering place but with those traveling merchants, the Yankee tin peddler.

In early New England in the foothills and rural backcountry was heard the familiar pronouncement, "Anything for the tin peddler today?" announcing the arrival of the itinerant merchant. There's was a hard life, setting out by cart just after mud season, and traveling through to the first snows, sleeping at taverns and in haylofts, and replenishing their stock at wholesale merchants along the way.

"Scuttles and cans, buttons and bows, I'll cure your ills, and cheer your woes!" cries the peddler, flashing his display of tinware and kitchen utensils, shirts and breeches, tobacco and pipes, pots and pans, hammers, matches, clothespins and washboards, glassware, notions and remedies, and other necessities of workaday life.

Back in these days before radio and good roads, the peddler also delivered news of the day to these remote homesteads and farms. Further, in order to while away the quiet hours, he also carried a line of popular authors such as Mark Twain, Louisa May Alcott, and Nathaniel Hawthorne, and practical tomes like the *Holy Bible*, *Science & Health*, and *The Boston Cookbook*.

The transactions were generally conducted by trade — the foremost commodity for which were rags, particularly white ones, weighed by the pound. Also, iron, copper, pewter, pelts, and beeswax served as exchange. And it was by both necessity and sport that a trade was initiated — no matter how reluctant the customer.

One of the most prosperous peddlers of the nineteenth century was Lon Newton of Rutland, Vermont who kept a journal in which he records that he once started a trade on the slimmest of pretexts and based on the tallest of tales:

> "I've got wooden nutmegs, pocket sawmills," says I, "and basswood hams, calico hog troths, white oak cheeses, and various other articles too numerous to mention." The old man just shook his head. He was so confident he warn't going to trade, that I made up my mind he'd got to. I saw a pair of old boots, and I said them was just what I wanted.
>
> "What?" he says, "d'ye buy old boots?" And I said them was my particuler specialty. "How much d'yer give?"
>
> "Half a cent a pound s'longs half cent's a coin," says I. He didn't take no heed to my meaning but began to rummage around and git out three or four pair. They weren't no good to me, but I was starting a trade. "Now, h'ain't yer got some rags?" Them was what I asked for first, and the old feller said he didn't have none; but now stirred up by the chanst of gitting something for his old boots, he brought out seventeen pounds of rags, and we did a brisk bit of trading for tinware. I left the old boots sitting beside the gate when I drove away. Them will come in handy to start another trade on, next time I come.

☛ John Calvin Coolidge was born on July 4, 1872 in Plymouth Notch, Vermont. In his youth Cal, as he was known, spent time at his father's country store, and undoubtedly it was here he picked up his legendary sharp wit and thrift in all matters including language. "I was never hurt by anything I didn't say," he once commented. He attended Amherst College in Northampton, Massachusetts where he eventually practiced law and entered Republican politics, first becoming a councilman, next a state senator, and then governor.

It was during the Boston police strike of 1919 that he earned his reputation for decisive action. "There is no right to strike against the public safety by anybody, anywhere, anytime," he wrote in a telegram. This seminal event brought him national attention and the vice presidency under Warren G. Harding.

Despite a career that took him first to Northampton, then Boston, and finally to Washington, Mr. Coolidge never strayed too far from his home state. In an impromptu speech he told a crowd in Bennington:

> It was here that I first saw the light of day; here that I received my bride; here my dead lie pillowed on the loving breast of our everlasting hills. I love Vermont most of all because of her indomitable people. If the spirit of liberty should vanish in other parts of the union and support of our institutions should languish, it could all be replenished from the generous store held by the people of this brave little state.

On August 3, 1923 while vacationing in Vermont, Vice President Coolidge learned of President Harding's sudden death. So at 2:47 in the morning by the light of a kerosene lamp, his father, who served as notary public, administered the oath of presidency as Mr. Coolidge held his hand on the family Bible. After the swearing in, someone suggested they commemorate the occasion with a drink, so they walked to his father's country store and swigged Moxie, a soft beverage.

It was in those subsequent years that President Coolidge earned the moniker, Silent Cal. "No man ever listened himself out of a job," he said. But to some, his Yankee demeanor was something of an affront. Teddy Roosevelt's daughter, Alice, once commented, "He looks like he was weaned on a pickle."

Of all his quotable philosophies, Silent Cal's most enduring homily, perhaps, was the one entitled "Press On":

> Nothing in the world can take the place of persistence. Talent will not — nothing is more common than unsuccessful men with talent. Genius will not — unrewarded genius is almost a proverb. Education will not — the world is full of educated derelicts. Persistence and determination alone are omnipotent.

On January 5, 1933 a decade after his swearing in, the retired president breathed his last and was buried in the town cemetery in Plymouth Notch. Despite his humble beginning and subsequent achievements, Mr. Coolidge was typically blunt. "Prosperity is only an instrument to be used," he said, "not a deity to be worshipped."

The She-Bear

In the springtime after bears emerge from hibernation and are at their lowest weight, they're darned hungry, as you might expect. Since berries, a bear's equivalent to Ben and Jerry's ice cream, aren't yet in season, these critters pretty much have to satisfy their cravings with main course fare.

Spud Carpenter is a potato farmer over by Arrow Lake and with his wife, Isabelle, keeps a few chickens, several pigs, and some cows. Well, something's been getting his "shorts", the young pigs, so he put his dog, Liberty, out there as watchdog. Problem is, after he and Isabelle went to bed, Libby went into the barn and fell asleep.

Determined to figure out what's invading his pen, Spud sets a lantern on the post out there and sits up late watching. Shutting off the kitchen lamp, he pokes his shotgun out the window, and as the Regulator clock in the parlor ticks away the time he waits and waits. Spud's telling this to some of the fellahs sitting around the potbelly woodstove in Bill Peterson's Country Store.

"At about the time the half moon begins to rise behind Sugar Hill," Spud's saying, "I spot something moving down by the tree line at the far end of the potato field. It hesitates a spell, then it slowly moved in toward the pig gate."

"Godfrey," says Henry Foster, "Could you tell who it was?"

"After my eyes kinda adjusted, I could see it was a great she-bear, and she had a short tucked up under one arm."

"You sure it warn't Josiah or one of his brood?" inquires Fred Johnson, who owns the Richfield filling station and garage in town.

"No sir, it were a bear," Spud insists, "and I notice she had sort of a white rosette on her brow, so I take careful aim and am about to squeeze the trigger, when that old bear, she just turns her head, glares at me, then blows out that light."

Your Dog Bite?

Sometime back a spell Bill Peterson stepped out onto the porch and notices Josiah Coates's old dog, Dawg, just sprawled out there in the sun. About then a car pulls in front, and it turns out to be the salesman from Greene Distributing Company, the concern that supplies Bill with most of the dry goods in his store.

"Your dog bite?" the salesman shouts from the open car window.

"Never has," Bill hollers back. So the salesman steps out of his car and walks over to pat Dawg on the head. Dawg, though, sensing he has a stranger in his sights, leaps up and chases that salesman up the porch stairs and into the safety of Bill's store.

"I thought you told me your dog doesn't bite," the salesman hollers at Bill.

"Mine never has," Bill tells him.

The German Visitor

There's a summer fellah who has a cabin up Moose Head Trail. He's been retired some years and spends most of his time riding his horse up the backcountry over behind Sugar Hill. This fellah's of German background with considerable Prussian traits, so you know when he rides, he rides the horse hard.

Enoch Webster was up to Bill Peterson's Country Store t'other afternoon sitting on the porch when this German fellah reins up his horse and leaps off.

"Watch my horse," he shouts at Enoch and marches inside. Some time passes before he eventually comes out again, but by now there's no horse. "I thought I told you to watch my horse," he shouts at Enoch.

"Gawd, I did," Enoch tells him, "He's down there now just going past the bank."

What's That Noise?

Junior Coates comes down to Bill Peterson's Country Store. Seems he's agreed to cut logs for the Northwood Paper Company on their land up Granite Mountain, so he's come down to Bill's to buy himself a saw.

"You'll have a damsite easier job of it, if you use one of these new chainsaws," Bill tells him. So Junior purchases one and heads out. After a spell of a month or so, Junior shows back, and he's dog tired from all the work he's doing up the mountain.

"That logging job's wearing you out," Bill says, as Junior drags his tired frame into the store.

"It's not bad," Junior tells him, "but it sure is rugged work."

"It'd have been worse without that chainsaw," Bill comments.

"I give that up," Junior replies.

"Why'd you do that?" Bill wants to know.

"It's just easier with the saw I got," Junior says.

"That rusty chunk of sheet metal?" Bill asks, "What's wrong with the chainsaw I sold you?"

"Too heavy and slow," Junior responds, "I got it out in the wagon."

"Bring it in and let's have a look at it," Bill tells him.

After Junior fetches the chainsaw and comes back in, Bill can see it'd hardly been used, so he tugs the cord, and the chainsaw starts right up just as nice as you please.

"Dang," says Junior, "What's that noise?"

She Scatters

To grasp this story first you need to know there was a time when homes, particularly rural homes, didn't have indoor plumbing save, perhaps, a well pump in the kitchen sink. So in order to tend to nature's call, you'd have to trot down a well-worn path to the outhouse situated someplace beyond odor range and away from the well.

That was okay in summer, but with New England's harsh winters, most nights you'd hold it until daybreak — that is, unless you had a chamber pot under the bed to serve those times of nocturnal necessity. Horace Peckham is in Bill Peterson's Country Store preparing to make such an acquisition.

"Bill," Horace says with hushed voice, "I need to buy a pot."

"Bean pot?" Bill asks.

"You know," Horace says, "A chamber pot."

So Bill goes out to the back room, then returns, setting the little pot on the counter.

"Here you go, Horace," Bill says, "This ought to do it for you."

"That's a fine pot," Horace says, "but ain't it a mite small?"

"I got a larger pot, if you want to see it," Bill states, going back, fetching another, and returning, setting the second pot next to the first.

"It's a nice pot with a good handle," he says, "and it's got a soft lip — can't see what else you'd want than that."

"It's a pretty good pot," Horace agrees, "but there's just one thing — it's a mite small still, ain't it?"

"Gawd, what d'ya want?" Bill wants to know, as he goes out back again for another. "Here you are, Horace," Bill declares upon his return, "This ought to fit that tail end of yours."

"Now, there's no point getting touchy," Horace rebukes, "If it were for me, that first one would be just fine. But it's for Eileen, and that woman scatters something wicked."

Josiah's Skunk

Sometime after ol' Dawg was put down, Josiah Coates comes into Bill Peterson's Country Store to purchase a sack of cat food.

"You trying out a cat this time?" Bill inquires mostly to make conversation, and to try to keep his mind from the fact it'd been a spell since Josiah had last been down the river for a bath.

"No, sir," says Josiah, "I got me a skunk."

"A skunk?" Bill says, "Where you keeping it?"

"Up my trailer," Josiah tells him.

"Gawd," Bill exclaims, "What about the stink?"

"He don't complain," Josiah replies.

The Thanksgiving Turkey

If New England owns any holiday, it's Thanksgiving — a secular remembrance of a religious feast first celebrated by the Wampanoag natives and Pilgrim settlers in 1621. Initially, this celebration was a tribute to the Great Spirit God for His many blessings, however as it's evolved, the feast is now an annual gathering followed by three days of turkey leftovers.

It'd been a particularly active business day the Wednesday before Thanksgiving when Dr. Robert Kenny saunters into Bill Peterson's Country Store and ambles over to the meat case where there's but one turkey left.

Dr. Kenny is the town physician who keeps normal office hours at his house in Center Northwood but as often as not is seen driving his Packard coupe about, restoring health to the housebound of the surrounding hills.

"Are you sure that's a turkey?" Dr. Kenny inquires.

"Of course it is," Bill replies.

This turkey, you must know, is the scrawniest bird anyone has ever seen. The doctor stares at it a mite, then look up at Bill.

"What it needed was treatment," Dr. Kenny says, "but you just let it run down."

Fish Chowder

It's unseasonably hot Saturday when Junior hauls his wagon up to Bill Peterson's Country Store. He's stopped to fetch a bag each of potatoes and onions.

"What's the stink?" asks Enoch Webster, who's sitting on the porch bench marked "Republicans".

"Fish scraps from the cove," Junior shouts above the drone of the flies. His wagon has dripped a trail of reeking fish juice from

Snug Harbour to Bill's steps and is now making a puddle in the road.

"You better bury that muck," Enoch advises.

"I'm heading up my father's," Junior says.

"Not surprised," Enoch replies.

"We're feeding this to his cows," Junior continues, "Then we'll milk them, slice in potatoes and onions, and make chowder."

"What you make are a couple chowderheads," Enoch comments.

Junior doesn't often express anger, but this time he makes an exception.

"Dang it!" he fumes, "T'ain't nothing 'tween you and a fool!"

"Just the rail of this porch," Enoch replies.

5.
The Church

THE CHURCH FIGURES PROMINENTLY in New England stories mainly because the church figures prominently in New England's heritage. Early civic government was usually run from the church meetinghouse.

By "church" what's meant is the Congregational Church, which with typical New England independence is fully run by the members with the minister being the hired hand. No representative elders, bishops, or priests. Even today many New England towns use the congregational style of governance — town meetings introduced to counter the perception of a ruling class over commoners.

New England was founded by two groups of conservative English Puritans, Protestants who prefer "pure" scriptural instruction to the dogmatic teachings of the Church of England. The Pilgrims, as we know them, settled in what they named Plimoth Plantation on the South Shore near Cape Cod, and the Puritans of Salem settled on the North Shore near Cape Ann.

The first New England towns were established as commercial expansions of these communities with entrepreneurial governors and a board of village selectmen administrating at the town meeting house on workdays and the minister conducting worship services on Sunday.

Eventually in 1636, there was a merger-of-necessity when the Pilgrims and the Salem Puritans established an academy of higher learning to educate young men into the clergy. This merged Protestant assembly is the Congregational Church, and the academy is the Harvard Divinity School, though New England Unitarians have pretty much taken over.

☛ In the 1800's, collectivism among New England Protestants was running rampant, at least in regards to communal living and abstinence from privacy and other personal matters.

Fifteen disciples of Ralph Waldo Emerson established a Christian commune called Brook Farm in West Roxbury, Massachusetts. George Ripley was their leader, and in his manifesto he stated that they sought individual freedom and humane relationships — so they got up at the crack of dawn, performed laborious tasks, and assumed God, "the Supreme Economist", would cash all this in as happiness and riches. Naturally, their strict rules thwarted individual freedom and humane comforts, and soon the whole farm went to seed.

Elsewhere in New England similarly minded Protestants, the so-called Shakers for their demonstrative ways, were celibate followers of Ann Lee, an English woman whose four children had died in infancy putting her off male-female relationships. In its day there were Shaker farm communes in Massachusetts, Connecticut, New Hampshire, Maine, and elsewhere — however as a group, the Shakers are best known among "the world's people" for their utilitarian furniture, innovative kitchen utensils, and imaginative farm equipment. But even Mother Ann could foresee the futility of a celibate community. "There will come a time," she wrote, "when there won't be enough Believers to bury their own dead."

As far as we know, there are but two Shakers left today at Sabbathday Lake, Maine.

You Broke My Cookies

The Reverend Preston Powell is our new minister, though his start here last autumn was somewhat unfortunate. It was Halloween when he, his wife, Patience, and their little girl, Gracie, settle into the parsonage behind the Congregational Meeting House. Because they'd just arrived, it isn't until trick or treat time that folks up to the Center get to meet the young family.

As they make the rounds house-to-house with their little girl all dressed pretty in her frilly white angel costume and big bag of treats, they came to Edna Phelps's house. Edna, being a lifelong parishioner, she's eager to make a favorable impression. Selecting the largest apple in her bowl of carefully wrapped caramel apples, Edna drops it into Gracie's big treats bag.

Well sir, that little girl looks down all wide-eyed into her treats bag then up at Edna with utter surprise on her sweet, childish face and says, "You sonuvabitch, you broke my cookies."

The Man Couldn't Swim

Young seminarians, as they begin their journey winning souls for the Lord, often become overwhelmed not just by the Holy Spirit but also by the enthusiasm of youth. Tom Lillibridge came upon one such novice passing out tracts at the corner by the bank.

"Have you found Jesus?" the novice asks him.

"Gawd," says Tom, "I didn't know he was lost."

Not the response expected, but persuading Yankees can be a risky endeavor, as the Reverend Powell discovers.

That first summer after he and his family arrived, Preston Powell fancies taking his faith into the community, so he sets up a large revival tent in the gravel parking area down Snug Harbour.

That night as he stands at the pulpit with a mixture of enthusiasm tempered by a degree of apprehension, he gazes over those gathered — this group doesn't have the look of a typical Christian assembly.

Since his audience is primarily young fellahs from the docks, the Reverend Powell senses he might make better progress if he mentions Jesus was a friend of fishermen. This eventually leads to the miracle of Christ walking on the water, so he leans toward his flock and asks, "Does anyone know *why* Jesus walked on the water?"

There's an awkward silence as eyes cast downward, then suddenly Matt Conley, who has the odor of having just strung bait, stands up. "I don't know this Jesus fellah," he says, "but I'm willing to bet the man couldn't swim."

Not According To Scripture

During the last war, Josiah Coates had been serving in the Army, which in its wisdom kept him and one other fellah far from the front line figuring to keep the casualty statistics down by at least two.

One afternoon Josiah and the fellah are assigned to dig a hole into which they're to sink a beast of burden that had died pulling a caisson. While they're digging, they're arguing about whether the critter is a mule or a donkey when the chaplain comes by and inquires what the quarrel is about.

"Boys", the chaplain advises diplomatically, "According to scripture, that particular creature is called an 'ass,'" then he goes away.

After another hour of digging and sweating, a sergeant comes along and asks what they are up to.

"Just digging a hole according to orders, sir," Josiah tells him.

"This isn't supposed to be a foxhole, is it?" the sergeant asks.

"Not according to scripture, sir," Josiah says.

Uncut Homily

The weekend after his arrival with his family to the parsonage up Center Northwood, the Reverend Preston Powell delivers his first sermon with a large bandage glued to his chin.

"I apologize for my appearance," he says to the congregation, "As I was shaving, I was concentrating on what I wanted to say to you this morning." He then commences to give a homily that comes right out of the old-time Puritan tradition of having too many themes and taking far too long.

After he finally wraps up and many of the ladies rush out and down the road to tend to overdone pot roasts, the Reverend Powell stands by the front door shaking hands and asking, "How'd it go?" That question alone causing most of his flock to break Commandment IX about not lying. That is, except Walt Palmer.

"So, what'd you think, Mr. Palmer?" the minister asks.

"Well, sir, I have but one thought," Walt tells him.

"What's that?" the Reverend Powell inquires.

"Next week," Walt tells him, "you'll be a damsite better off if you concentrate on your face and cut your sermon."

Jesus Shoes

As the country started into "The Great War", the government employed "spotters" along the New England coast. These fellahs were responsible for scrutinizing the North Atlantic horizon for enemy ships, and periodically calling in their reports. Lookout towers were built in haste using the materials at hand. Some were fairly rugged, built of lumber and painted, while others were merely log poles bolted together, looking somewhat like a deer stand hunters use.

Walt Palmer is a lifelong commercial fisherman, so he reckons what with his expertise at sea, he should sign up as a coast spotter. Late one afternoon as evening approaches Walt is up in his perch when he spies what he thinks is a freighter running a distance offshore. Not sure what he's seeing, Walt calls in a report that is fairly sketchy given the darkness of the hour.

"All I can see is the port light," Walt reports to the lieutenant on duty, "and I can just make out the light on her mast."

"What's her tonnage?" asks the lieutenant.

"Godfrey," he replies, "It's dark out here, you know."

"Can you see markings on her stack?" the lieutenant wants to know, "What color is it?"

"Like I say," Walt tells him, "it's wicked dark."

"We're going to need more than that," the lieutenant insists.

"What the hell you want me to do?" asks Walt, "Put on my Jesus shoes and walk around her?"

The Whole Damn Load

In upcountry New England there are small churches whose congregations are too small to support a full-time minister, so the denomination sends a parson around on a periodic basis to support the lay ministry and to deliver a message.

It's spring sugaring time and the sap buckets are hanging from the maples as the Reverend Powell makes his way up through the rutted dirt trails passing for roads to a little church — a strong, sweet air drifting from a nearby sugarhouse.

On this occasion, though, what with everyone engaged in sugaring, he arrives to find a lone parishioner stoking the woodstove, no one else having shown up. Not sure how to proceed, he asks the parishioner what they might do.

"I'm just a farmer," the parishioner says, "but if I load some hay in the wagon to go out to feed my cows and only one cow shows up, I feed her."

Taking the point, the Reverend Powell carries on full bore with the sermon just as he'd prepared it. After he'd concluded, curious on how it went, he asks the lone parishioner what he thought.

"Well, like I told you, I'm just a farmer," he replies, "but if I load some hay into the wagon to go out to feed the cows and only one cow shows up, I don't give her the whole damn load."

Two or Three Steps

Matt Conley's never been a particularly religious fellah, but ever since he heard the Reverend Powell preaching on Jesus walking upon the water, Matt's been pondering the story — kind of consumed by it, you might say.

One morning after the fog lifted, Matt decides to drive down Snug Harbour to that stretch of shore over by Fish's Dock. After staring over the ripples coming onto the beach, Matt, dressed in a flannel shirt and dungarees, runs into the water right up to his knees.

Walt Palmer is just pulling into the gravel parking area with his horse and wagon when he sees Matt running into the cove. Now, Walt's a fairly religious fellah himself, you know, so after he'd jumped down and approached the beach, he shouts to Matt, "How's the water?"

"Not bad, not bad at all," Matt hollers back, "I took two or three steps before I went down."

Taking Up Music

Music is an expressive element of worship — in the here and now and in life everlasting scripture tells us. In colonial New England when singing was accompanied by limited instrumentation, if any, and churches were stark and naturally acoustical, a style of hymn singing developed called "sacred harp", which helped tone-challenged congregations master harmony.

During the weekly hymn sing, the leader would arrange the chairs so the altos, sopranos, basses, and tenors could sit across from each other in what they called a "hollow square". Each group would then take turns leading the singing.

There's also harp singing of a different sort — performed by angels, saints, and the heavenly hosts singing in divine perfection and on key. It's this type of singing Enoch Webster's thinking about the day the census enumerator came around.

"How old are you, Mr. Webster," the enumerator asks.

"I'm ninety-six," he tells her.

"My goodness," she responds, then kinda unofficially asks, "What do you see yourself doing when you reach one hundred?"

"I think by then I might take up music," he replies.

Hand It To Him Myself

Walt Palmer, you know, is a pretty religious fellah who's also a particularly cautious steward of money. He attends services up to the Congregational Meeting House, and last Sunday the Reverend Powell took Walt aside during the coffee and fellowship time.

"I notice by our records," the minister tells him, "you haven't given an offering in quite some time."

"I believe you're correct," Walt agrees.

"Don't you think you ought be giving something to the Lord?" he inquires.

"How old are you?" Walt asks.

"I'm thirty-two," Reverend Powell replies, "but I don't see..."

"Well, I'm seventy-eight," Walt tells him, "and don't you suppose I'll pass on before you do?"

"Well, yes, I suppose," the minister admits.

"So I'll see the Lord before you will?" Walt asks.

"I suppose," he consents.

"Then I think I'll wait and hand it to him myself," Walt replies.

Not Today, Thank You

Last Christmas eve as he begins speaking, the Reverend Powell, filled with the Holy Spirit and enthused by the season, notices folks among the gathered he hasn't seen since Easter.

"T'was this time years ago that a new life intervened in our world," he exclaims, "a life proclaiming eternal life for all who accepts it!"

Then he lets loose with an evangelical message unlike anything this assembly of frozen chosen has ever heard.

"Today you, too, can claim this new life, this eternal life!" Reverend Powell cries, taking a turn no New England preacher usually would.

"Who among us this evening wants to go to heaven?" he demands, "Come, stand, if you want to be counted among those sitting in the glow of God's eternal grace and glory!"

New Englanders are pretty reluctant to let anyone know their business, so such a public proclamation causes no little consternation, to be sure. Slowly though, everyone to a man stands, save one.

"What's the matter, Miss Phelps?" he asks Edna, who's the lone holdout, "Don't you want to go to heaven, too?"

"Not today, thank you," Edna replies, "I'm expecting company."

The Quahaug Quartet

For the most part there are two types of clamming done in New England. Fellahs going out for soft shell clams, the small clams usually steamed and served with melted butter, will use a clam rake to dig them from the dark muck of coastal clam-flats at low tide. Other fellahs, though, wanting hard shell clams, what the native New Englanders call *quahogs* and are quite often used in chowder, will set out in their skiffs and using a set of tongs, dig them from the bottom of small coves. Walt Palmer's down Salt Cove in his skiff tonging when he hears a hum emitting from the galvanized basket of clams he's already collected. He starts sorting through the basket trying to figure out what's causing this, when he discovers it's from the clams themselves.

After he'd tonged half a bushel or so, and the hum's become fairly loud, Walt strikes upon an inspiration that he believes can only be heaven sent. He sorts through the basket again locating an alto, soprano, bass, and tenor, then he loads some bottom muck into a wooden fish box and positions the clams, sort of tucking them in. Over the next several months of impassioned training, he eventually succeeds in getting his little clams to harmonize his favorite hymn, "Blessed Assurance".

At their debut recital at the Congregational Meeting House — outside where the clam muck won't stink up the sanctuary — the Palmer Quahaug Quartet, as he's named them, is a harmonic sensation. Word spreads and soon Walt and his humming clams are touring area churches, even giving a "clammand performance" down the Rumford Falls Town House.

Amid all this, Walt receives an invitation from the Rose Island Baptist Church to perform out there. On the morning of the recital, Walt loads his box of clams into his smack, DAUNTLESS, and sets off for the island. It's windy and spitting rain, so when they get around Cod Point the swell kicks up something wicked, and his clams take sick and die. Later, back at the Congregational Meeting House, Walt reports about his trip out to the Baptist Church and the sad events of that day.

"Don't know if t'was the swell that done it," Walt tells those assembled, "or that the Almighty is thoroughly Congregational."

6.
Grave Humor

THROUGHOUT NEW ENGLAND in cities, in towns, and in tiny villages, which survive in name alone, are ancient burial grounds remembered by some but mostly forgotten.

Perhaps the most treasured Yankee cemetery is the historic Granary Burial Ground in Boston. Among the celebrities planted there are John Hancock, Samuel Adams, Paul Revere, Elizabeth "Mother" Goose, and Cripus Attucks, the first Black victim of the American Revolution.

Throughout the region there are similar, though less renown, churchyards whose inhabitants aren't famous but who are nonetheless remembered primarily for their wit — or the wit of their survivors — as evidenced by the stones o'er their graves.

A grave in Eastham, Massachusetts offers this sobering observation:

> AS YOU PASS BY
> AND CAST AN EYE,
> AS YOU ARE NOW,
> SO ONCE WAS I.

In Lincoln, Maine this granite declaration is perhaps the first personals advertisement in the New World:

> SACRED TO THE MEMORY OF JARED BATES,
> WHO DIED AUGUST THE 6TH, 1800.
> HIS WIDOW, AGED 24, LIVES AT 7 ELM STREET,
> HAS EVERY QUALIFICATION FOR A GOOD WIFE
> AND LONGS TO BE COMFORTED.

Over in East Derry, New Hampshire there's this simple inscription that seems almost rueful:

> I TOLD YOU I WAS SICK.

And then there's this farmer's lament from up in Orford, New Hampshire:

> TO ALL MY FRIENDS
> I BID ADIEU,
> A MORE SUDDEN DEATH
> YOU NEVER KNEW.
> AS I WAS LEADING
> THE MARE TO DRINK,
> SHE KICKED AND KILLED ME
> AS QUICK AS A WINK.

And in a final word regarding his late misses, an apparently long-suffering husband in Hatfield, Massachusetts had engraved on her stone:

> 1771.
> HERE LIES SILENT AS CLAY
> MISS ARABELLA YOUNG
> WHO ON THE 21ST OF MAY
> BEGAN TO HOLD HER TONGUE.

☛ Possibly the most infamous deaths in New England were those of wealthy banker Andrew Borden and his second wife on August 4, 1892 in Fall River, Massachusetts. This bloody double homicide is remembered not so much for the victims but for the victims' daughter, Lizzie.

Her much publicized murder trial revealed family dissention regarding inheritance — her stepmother's family was disfavored — and that Lizzie had burned the bloodstained clothing of her father and stepmother in the kitchen stove.

In the years since there have been numerous books, an opera, a ballet, and even a little ditty that has been recited by schoolchildren for generations:

> *Lizzie Borden took an ax,*
> *And gave her mother forty whacks.*
> *When she saw what she had done,*
> *She gave her father forty-one.*

Although shunned by the community, Lizzie was acquitted, and she and her older sister retained the Borden inheritance. Today the family's Victorian home on Second Street is a bed and breakfast inn and gift shop.

Up To the Cemetery

There was once a time in New England when societal decorum dictated certain matters of trade be handled in a gender specific way, and so it is when a woman tourist steps up to the counter in Bill Peterson's Country Store.

"May I speak to the lady of the store?" the woman asks.

"She's not here," Bill tells her.

"I believe I shall wait for her," the woman replies.

After a half an hour, the woman is becoming a mite edgy, so she again steps up to the counter.

"I have been waiting an unreasonably long time, Mr. Peterson," she states emphatically, "Where do you suppose your wife is?"

"She's up to the cemetery," Bill says.

"When do you believe she'll be back?" the woman wants to know.

"Well, she's been up there five years," Bill replies, "and I don't think she'll be returning anytime soon."

Gettin' Old

Edna Phelps down the Coast Road just turned ninety-one, and she's still living in the same house she built some seventy years ago. She never married, not that it ever slowed her down.

Just before her birthday *The Northwood Independent* sent a reporter around to interview her. When he arrived at her house, he notices a leaflet titled *Trusted Remedies For Memory Loss* setting on the sideboard.

"You concerned you're getting absentminded?" the reporter asks, pointing to the leaflet.

"Lordy, if I lose my mind," Edna tells him, "I don't believe I'll miss it none."

This question did set her to pondering, so before long Edna calls on Charley Snow down at his funeral parlor to makes arrangements beforehand. The preparations came together nicely, and Charley makes notations in his register regarding the style of the box and the shape of the stone, but when it comes to the inscription, Edna is particularly explicit.

"On the stone I don't want it to say 'Miss Edna Phelps,'" she tells him, "because I've lived ninety-one years, and I don't believe I've missed a thing."

Ol' Hattie

When she'd gotten on in years, Hattie Arnold was supposed to go live with her sister off Moose Head Trail. The both of them, you know, live alone.

"I don't think it'd hardly work out," she said of the arrangement. "You take my sister — she and I aren't no more alike than if it weren't us."

Finally, though, Roger Hancock's younger son, Kenny, had to drive her up the County Home, and she was feeling wicked grim about it.

"I suppose this is the last time I'll pass through town," she says to Kenny.

"You'll go through at least once more," Kenny tells her, "but it'll probably be feet first."

Aunt Emma's Funeral

Harry Babcock comes into Bill Peterson's Country Store dressed better than usual.

"What's the occasion?" Bill asks him.

"Burying," Harry says.

"You're picking berries in that getup?" Bill replies.

"My wife's Great Aunt Emma," Harry tells him, "Over to the burying ground."

It seems Aunt Emma had been down visiting friends when she took sick and died. Harry called down, had her crated and shipped back, but after she arrives, he looked in and discovered a frog's gotten into the works somehow.

"It seems we got us a major general in full dress uniform," Harry reports.

"What you figure on doing?" asks Bill, who's beside himself laughing.

"I'll tell you what I'm going to do," Harry says, "I'm not saying a damn thing, and we're going the plant this fellah and hope somewhere Aunt Emma's enjoying herself a twenty-one gun salute."

Kinda Peekid

George Hancock passed away in the autumn of 1909, but last summer the state had to dig him up again so they could straighten out the bend on North Road. Apparently there's a law someplace that says a relative has to be present, so his grandson, Joe, is chosen to represent the family. After they'd replanted the old fellah in the town burying ground, Joe heads home.

"How'd it go?" Roger, his father, inquires as he comes through the kitchen door.

"Not bad," replies Joe.

"You help with the diggin'?" Roger asks.

"Some," Joe answers.

"Was it hard?" Roger wants to know.

"It was packed kinda tight," Joe reports.

"Dirt?" Roger asks.

"Clay, mostly," Joe replies.

"How's the box?" Roger inquires.

"Wicked poor," Joe says.

"You look in?" Roger asks him.

"Yep," Joe answers.

"How was he?" Roger wants to know.

"Kinda peekid," Joe replies.

Up She Comes!

There are a lot of old folks up North Road, and they're always dying. It must be two months ago when Hattie Arnold finally passed away. She'd been up there at the County Home, you know, and that County Home sets way back there.

Tom Lillibridge, besides fishing with Walt Palmer, is also the town's gravedigger, so at the selectman's meeting, the moderator says to Tom, "We want you should go up there and put her under."

"It's pretty hard digging, all that gravel up there," Tom says, "and besides the frost's into the ground."

"You're the town gravedigger," he says to Tom, "and it's up to you to plant her."

Well sir, Tom gets up there, and it's mighty mean. The fellahs down Rumford Falls, when it gets too rugged, they bury them down the flat, but Tom would rather sink them in Arrow Lake as down that flat. Nonetheless, he finally gets the old lady into the ground.

When the selectman's meeting came around again last week, Tom got right up and says, "Mister moderator, I want ten dollars for digging that grave and filling it in."

"Now Tom," the moderator says, "You know that's town work, and seven dollars is what we pay."

"No, sir," says Tom, "Ten dollars is what I want, and ten dollars is what I'll get."

"That's wrong," the moderator replies, "You know it's seven, and that's all we'll pay."

"If you don't pay me my ten dollars," Tom tells him, "up she comes!"

The Body In the River

A couple fly fishermen were down Wood River when they found a body over by Miller's Dam. Right off folks thought it might be Josiah Coates, who likes to hang out by the trestle upstream, so Horace Peckham and Henry Foster drive up to that old trailer of his to see if he's there.

"Josiah, you here?" Horace shouts, banging on the door.

"Go away!" Josiah hollers from inside.

"It's me and Henry," Horace says.

"What if 'tis?" Josiah yells.

"Some fellahs found a body down the river," Henry says, "and we thought it might be you."

"Were he wearing a red flannel shirt?" Josiah asks.

"Gawd, that's what they said," Horace replies, "He was wearing a red flannel shirt."

"Were he wearing blue trousers?" Josiah wants to know.

"Blue pants, yep," Horace says, "Blue dungarees, they said."

"Rubber boots?" Josiah asks.

"That's right, he had on boots", says Henry.

"Was they high or low boots?" Josiah inquires.

"Low, I think," Horace replies.

"You sure?" Josiah shouts through the door.

"Now I remember," Henry says, "They were waders turned down low."

"Well," Josiah says, "I guess it ain't me."

At the Burying Ground

Tom Lillibridge is trimming around the headstones while Jeremiah Coates is pushing the town's lawn mower, though he mows the crookedest row you've ever seen. In addition to being the town gravedigger, Tom also keeps the town burying ground next to the Congregational Meeting House, and he gets the use of Jeremiah because Judge Pratt has the boy on work detail most of the time.

Tom's grading around George Hancock's new stone as Enoch Webster strolls up with some unappreciated sidewalk observations.

"I watched them bring him here," Enoch says.

"That so?" says Tom.

"And I think they got it too shallow," he continues.

"He ain't getting out," Tom replies.

Enoch's watching Jeremiah as he bumps into grave markers, nicking them at about the six-inch level.

"Most cemeteries got fences," Enoch comments.

"Those on the inside aren't getting out," Tom says, "and those on the outside aren't much in a rush to get in."

Just then Jeremiah quits mowing and walks over toward them.

"You're the oldest man in town, that right?" Jeremiah asks.

"So they say," Enoch replies.

"Y'know," he remarks, "it don't hardly pay for you to go home."

Fresh As a Haddock

In her declining years, Isabelle Carpenter's mother had come to live with her and Spud on the farm. She was nearly deaf and spent most of her days sitting in a rocking chair next to the cookstove. Edna Phelps used to drop by on occasion to cheer her up — not that the old lady heard too much, but she enjoyed the company.

Last week Edna dropped by as she does, and not seeing the old lady, Edna inquires after her. "She's passed on," Isabelle tells her, but just then Edna notices a strange look come over Spud's face.

"Godfrey," he says, "She's still in the shed."

There'd been snow on the ground when Isabelle's mother died, so Spud built a box for her, then set her in the woodshed, waiting for a thaw when he could dig the hole. Eventually, Spud kinda forgot about it and had Junior Coates come down to load wood into the shed.

Spud hurriedly calls Junior, and in no time the two of them were tossing back firewood. After they'd hefted out the box, Spud thought somebody ought to check, so Junior opens the lid and peeks in.

"How she look?" Spud inquires.

"You know," Junior says, "She's just as fresh as a haddock."

Fish's Dock down in Snug Harbour.

Bert & I

DESPITE THE POPULARITY OF YANKEE STORYTELLING during the early part of the twentieth century, at the half-century interest had all but disappeared. By the 1950's people were getting their entertainment in a can from radio, television, and motion pictures. Front porches where neighbors once shared stories had surrendered to backyard decks and patios. And the proprietor-run country stores where townsfolk swapped tales had submitted to self-serve IGA and chain supermarkets. Yankee humor as a folk art was essentially dead, or it would have been had it not been for two young fellahs attending Yale University in New Haven, Connecticut.

Robert Bryan and Marshall Dodge met as students and began sharing their passion for the oral traditions of northern New England. Not old enough to have experienced this folklore firsthand, they did possess an keen aptitude for retelling these tales to a new generation, so in 1959 they transcribed a collection of New England stories on a phonograph record called "Bert and I and Other Stories From Down East."

These stories along with the dialect and with vocal sound effects became such a sensation that in 1961 they recorded "More Bert and I and Other Stories From Down East". That led to over one hundred radio commercials in dialect for B&M Baked Beans and Air France. This was followed by the release of "The Return Of Bert and I", "Bert and I Stem Inflation", and "Bert and I On Stage".

It's been another half-century since the birth of Bert and I at Mother Yale, but the boys have followed a stalwart path during these intervening years:

Using his share of the proceeds, the Reverend Robert Bryan from his church in Ipswich, Massachusetts founded an outreach ministry in Northern Québec and Labrador, Canada.

Marshall Dodge, an adopted son of Maine, followed a duel career in philosophy and stage monologues until his accidental death in 1982, while bicycling in Hawai'i.

And the popularity of the Bert and I phonograph records continues, having yielded first to cassette tapes and now to compact discs.

7.
Patent Medicine

IN THE EARLY DAYS home healthcare included lozenges made from horehound leaves, drops from slippery elm bark, and syrup from licorice root. Soon entrepreneurs were packaging these remedies and selling them as cures for nearly every discomfort known to man and beast.

"Dr. Miller's Vegetable Expectorant", for instance, was formulated by E. Morgan & Sons in Providence, Rhode Island as a cure for "coughs, colds, and all lung troubles."

"Persian Pills," another vegetable treatment, was advertised as "the sovereign power over disease" and was sold by Henry Benton from his Hartford, Connecticut *bookstore.*

A few of these classic medicines are still around, though some of them are marketed today as homeopathic remedies:

LYDIA PINKHAM'S VEGETABLE COMPOUND, founded in Lynn, Massachusetts in 1875 and prepared with natural ingredients, and alcohol, is sold "for all those painful complaints and weaknesses so common to our best female population."

SLOAN'S LINIMENT was founded in 1871 by "Doctor" Earl S. Sloan — not actually a doctor — who manufactured this camphor and menthol cream in Boston and marketed it as "the relief from aches and pains of the joints and muscles."

DICKENSON'S WITCH HAZEL, an astringent originated in 1866 by Thomas Newton Dickinson in Essex, Connecticut, is distilled from native witch hazel shrubs and is sold today for "a gentle, more natural, skin care regimen."

FATHER JOHN'S MEDICINE, comprising cod liver oil and licorice extract, was first formulated in a Lowell, Massachusetts apothecary in 1855. Favored by the parish priest, John O'Brien, because it contains no alcohol, the tonic is still marketed with Father John's picture for "consumption, grippe, croup, whooping cough, and other diseases of the throat."

TUTTLE'S ELIXIR was founded in 1885 by Samuel A. Tuttle and manufactured in Boston as the cure for rheumatism, sprains, stiff joints, and frozen feet. Today this remedy is sold as a veterinary salve.

THAYER'S SLIPPERY ELM LOZENGES, originating in Cambridge, Massachusetts in 1847 by Dr. Henry Thayer, became popular with scratchy-throated church choirs, and is still marketed as "an old-fashioned, all natural remedy."

Although Dr. Thayer's lozenges are made of natural ingredients, they may not be popular with *all* church choirs — don't know if the Christian Scientists go for them.

☛ Mary Baker Eddy, who founded what is now the Church of Christ, Scientist, was born in 1821 on her family's farm in Bow, New Hampshire. Rural families in those years often shared time reading the *Holy Bible*, so in her early days as Miss Eddy advanced in her knowledge and talents, particularly in writing, she also increased her wisdom of scripture.

Later as a young adult, though, Miss Eddy took to poor health and began taking patient medicines and bathing in cold water according to the convention of that day. Throughout this ordeal when she was near death, Miss Eddy also continued reading the *Bible* and praying.

After she regained health completely and had gained a passion for biblical healing, Miss Eddy coined the term "Christian science" and in 1875 published a book, *Science and Health.*

One thing led to another as it often does, and Miss Eddy, going against the popular belief that women couldn't be educated, established a small *co-ed* college in 1881, built her first church in 1884, and started a newspaper in 1908 "to injure no man, but to bless all mankind."

Today both the Mother Church of the worldwide Church of Christ, Scientist and its Pulitzer Prize-winning *The Christian Science Monitor* are located on the Christian Science campus in Boston.

The Party Line

During the first half of the twentieth century, the New England Telephone Company put people in rural areas on "party lines", meaning you shared the cable running along your road with other families. For that reason, each telephone call had a distinctive ring — your calls, for instance, might be identified by a short and a long ring-ringgggg, whereas your neighbor's calls might be identified by three short ring-ring-ring. Naturally, if your telephone sounds off but it's not your ring, you're supposed to leave it and give the other family privacy. But it doesn't always happen that way.

Harry Babcock hears the telephone a-jangling, so he tunes in on it. It's Edna Phelps out on the Coast Road, and she's talking to the doctor, Dr. Robert Kenny, our town's physician.

"Yes?" Harry hears him say.

"I think I got some kind of trouble," Edna says, "and I don't know what it is."

Harry is telling this later to Ann Champlin, the waitress over to Lew Cottrell's Minuteman Diner.

"Is that so?" Dr. Kenny replies.

"It's a kind of ringing in my ears," Edna tells him.

"Yes?" he says.

"It's a kind of ringing, and it keeps on all the time," she continues, "I asked the neighbors, but they don't hear anything."

Enoch's Heart Attack

Enoch Webster was up to the doctor's. As our town physician, Dr. Kenny conducts regular clinic hours at an office off his house in Center Northwood, and Enoch's up there with some sort of ailment.

"Tell me," Dr. Kenny asks, "What're your symptoms?"

"I'm feeling a mite tizziky, Doc," Enoch tells him.

"I'm not sure I understand," the doctor says.

"I'm not sure either," Enoch replies, "but that's how I feel."

With that Dr. Kenny has him lie on the examination table, and after a preliminary examination, he's certain of the cause.

"You, my friend, have had a heart attack," Dr. Kenny tells him, "and I'm going to admit you immediately."

As he turns to write in the chart, Enoch slowly gets up from the table and starts out the door.

"You're a sick man," Dr. Kenny tells him, "and I must admit you to the hospital."

"Yes, I know," says Enoch, "but this is a considerable decision, Doc, and I need to go home and think this over a spell."

Lose My Suction

"You know Edna Phelps, who lives up the Coast Road?" Harry Babcock's saying. Some of the fellahs are sitting at the counter over Lew Cottrell's Minuteman Diner. It's half-raining and half-snowing as Harry and Mary come in.

"We drop in on her from time-to-time," Mary says, "especially in wintertime to see how she's doing."

"We get over there, and I see there's a pot of beans at the back of the stove," Harry says, "The oven door's open, and there's a pan of biscuits, too. 'Golly, Edna,' I said just to make conversation, 'You been doing some baking?'"

"It seems Patience Powell, the minister's wife, had been there," Mary says, "She'd brought them over."

"'I haven't been able to touch a single one of them beans,' Edna told us." Harry's telling this, imitating Edna's wobbly voice the best he can. "'It's them nerves in my throat,' Edna said, 'Every time I get ready to take in a spoonful, I get just so far from my mouth when them nerves start a-jumping, and I lose my suction.'"

A Pretty Good Job

Eileen Peckham is feeling a mite poorly, so she badgers Horace into taking her down to Dr. Kenny's during regular office hours. After the doctor conducts an examination, he scratches his head and turns to Horace.

"I must tell you, Horace," he says, "I'm not too pleased how your wife looks."

"I don't like it either, Doc," Horace tells him, "but she does a pretty good job with the children."

President Harding

Warren G. Harding was the twenty-ninth president of the United States. He was descended from New England Puritans, raised in a staunchly religious home, and ran as the Republican presidential candidate in 1920. Although personally honest, President Harding was nevertheless too trusting and is remembered consequently for his corrupt administration and the Teapot Dome oil scandal.

In 1923 while traveling throughout the western United States and Alaska, President Harding fell ill, died, and was succeeded by his vice-president, Calvin Coolidge of Vermont.

It was sometime after this when Roger Hancock was up Granite Mountain cutting firewood with old Seth Thayer. This was the winter before Seth fell off his barn roof and died. They'd been cutting for twenty minutes or so when all of a sudden old Seth rolls over in the snow, holds his stomach, and groans something wicked.

"Seth, what ails you?" asks Roger.

"I got the collywobbles, and I'm a-dying," Seth complains, "and I want you go down the mountain and tell the folks just how it was."

"Now, Seth," says Roger, "There's nothing wrong with you."

"Oh yes there is," Seth insists, "I'm a-finished."

"You stay right here," Roger tells him, and he goes up the mountain to where a sawmill used to be. He goes to where the kitchen was and finds an old jar of mustard. Roger then grabs an old glass tumbler, mixes it up half mustard and half water, then trundles back down to where old Seth's laying in the snow.

"Here you go," Roger says, "I got something that'll fix you up."

"It ain't no use," old Seth moans, "I'm a-through."

"Well, if you're a-through," Roger says, "There's but one thing I want you to do for me before you go."

"I should be glad to accommodate you," Seth says, and with that Roger takes the tumbler, pours it down old Seth's throat, and it comes right back up green all over the snow.

"If they'd done that for President Harding," Roger tells him, "He'd have been with us yet."

The Dirtiest Foot

It's said that Josiah Coates is so stupid, he can't count to twenty with his shoes on, but that's giving him too much credit. He is over to Dr. Kenny's with some sort of foot ailment. It'd been a couple years since he'd last been there with a similar complaint, and that time the doctor pulled a thumbtack out of his foot.

"How long has this tack been hurting you?" the doctor asked him on that occasion.

"Week, week and a half, maybe," Josiah said.

"Maybe you should take your socks off more often," Dr. Kenny advised.

Well as I say, Josiah's back, and again Dr. Kenny hauls off his boot and probes the sore.

"You know something?" the doctor declares, "This just might be the dirtiest foot in town."

"You think so?" Josiah brags, "then take off the other boot."

My Convenience

Because old Enoch Webster lives out there on his farm all by himself, the folks in town have been trying to convince him to put in a telephone.

"I don't want one of those damn things," Enoch gripes each time someone brings it up. Well, finally the Reverend Powell persuades him to at least have one installed in case of an emergency.

One morning Charley Snow figures he'll drive up there to see how Enoch's getting along. They're sitting there in the kitchen when the telephone sounds off — ring-ringgggg, ring-ringgggg, ring-ringgggg.

"Isn't that your ring?" Charley asks.

"Don't know but what 'tis," Enoch replies.

"Then why the hell don't you answer it?" Charley wants to know.

"Because, Charley," Enoch says, "I had that phone put in for *my* convenience."

The Bald Head

Fred Johnson runs the Richfield filling station and garage in Center Northwood, and as you'd expect, the fellahs like hanging around sharing news and talking sports. T'other morning Henry Foster's there sitting on a stack of tires; Joe Hancock's perched on a drum of Richlube motor oil; and Fred's standing, sipping a bottle of Moxie when Dr. Kenny, the town's physician, drops by to have his Packard coupe worked on.

"I was down to the State Hospital yesterday," the doctor was saying. The State Hospital is where they take the feebleminded who have no one to take them in.

"There were a couple of gentlemen outdoors with a nurse," Dr. Kenny tells them, "and one is quite bald headed. Well, just then a bird flies over and deposits a calling card on the bald gentleman's head."

"Godfrey," says Henry.

"Well, the nurse, feeling this might throw him off some, tells him she'll go inside and fetch some toilet paper," Dr. Kenny says, "so after she'd gone I heard the bald gentlemen say to his friend, 'What a damned fool she is; that bird will be half a mile away by the time she gets back.'"

Enoch's Phone Call

You remember the Reverend Powell finally talks Enoch Webster into putting in a telephone, not that he uses it all that much. Though he did decide to call his old Army buddy long distance. He jiggles the thingamabob, and the operator comes on.

"I want to call long distance," he tells the operator.

"It's very expensive," she informs him.

"Don't matter," he tells her, "I want to call Texas."

"What town?" she asks.

"Amarillo," he replies.

"How do you spell it?" she inquires.

"Gawd, if I knew that," Enoch says, "I would have written him a letter."

Castor Oil

Fred Johnson shuffles into Bill Peterson's Country Store looking wicked poorly and begins rummaging around the bottles, jars, and boxes on the patent medicine shelf.

"What can I get you, Fred?" Bill inquires.

"I got stoppage," Fred tells him, "Got something for it?"

"Take a quarter pound of cheese," Bill replies, "It ain't a remedy but a cure."

"What do you know about this castor oil?" Fred asks.

"You want to try out a bottle?" Bill wants to know.

"You think I'll be well enough to get up in the morning?" Fred asks.

"You better be," Bill replies.

Cabin Fever

Like his father before him, Junior Coates has sired quite a load of children, but lately he's having an unusually challenging time fulfilling his marital obligations. In fact Lulu's so irritated by the situation, she's the one who suggests Junior go down and see Dr. Kenny.

"So, you're having problems with your libido?" the doctor asks.

"I don't know about that," Junior admits, "but I ain't functioning too good."

"It's been a hard winter," Dr. Kenny says, "and I'm thinking maybe you're just not getting enough exercise." Then the doctor suggests Junior try running four or five miles a day and see if that doesn't bring his body back into line. "Call me in two weeks," Dr. Kenny adds, "so I can assess the situation."

After the fourteen days had passed, the doctor's phone sounds off. "You told me to call you," Junior says from the other end of the line.

"Yes, Junior," Dr. Kenny replies, "How are relations with your wife?"

"Not too good, Doc," Junior admits, "So far I've gone sixty miles, more or less, and now I'm practically down to Manchester."

8.
Politics & Primaries

AFTER WEATHER AND SPORTS, there's perhaps no topic more talked about at country stores and around town than politics. And it's perhaps because of this interest that New England is the most represented region of the United States. In contrast to, say Texas, which is much larger than New England, the Lone Star state has but two senators to New England's twelve.

It's no accident, either, that the first presidential primary is in New Hampshire, one of the smallest of these United States. At campaign time it's said if you haven't met each candidate at least twice, you've been housebound.

In New England, the Democrat party primarily took hold in the immigrant communities of eastern Massachusetts, Rhode Island, and parts of Connecticut. However, since most of these stories originated in the up-country Yankee areas, a region that was so staunchly Republican it was said "Democrats travel by night," Democrats often serve as the punchline.

Political drollery isn't limited to stories, either, as evidenced by New England's actual, though archaic, "Blue Laws":

☞ In Maine, you may be fined for leaving your Christmas decorations up past January 14th. And in Augusta, the state capital, it's illegal to stroll down the street playing a violin.

☞ In New Hampshire you may not tap your feet, nod your head, nor in any way keep time to music in a restaurant.

☞ In Vermont there's a law prohibiting underwater whistling.

☞ In Massachusetts no gorilla may ride in the backseat of a car. Also, Quakers and witches are banned, bullets may not be used as currency, and mourners at a wake may not eat more than three sandwiches. In Longmeadow it is illegal for two men to carry a bathtub across the Town Green. In Marlborough the detonation of a nuclear device within city limits is prohibited. And in Newton all residents are entitled to a free hog given by the mayor.

☞ In Providence, Rhode Island it's illegal to sell toothpaste and a toothbrush to the same customer on a Sunday, yet everyday it is illegal to throw pickle juice on a trolley.

☞ In Hartford, Connecticut you may not educate dogs. And in Waterbury beauticians are banned from humming, whistling, and singing while working with a customer.

☛ Back in 1996 a young fellah named John O'Brien made a motion picture in which Fred Tuttle, a potato farmer, plays himself as the winning candidate for the Vermont seat in the United States House of Representatives. His campaign slogan was, "I've spent time in the barn, now I want to spend time in the House."

After the movie was completed, Mr. O'Brien with all the promotional bravado of that real New England politician, P. T. Barnum, talked Mr. Tuttle into running in the Republican primary as an official candidate.

Fred won.

What started off as a spoof to promote the motion picture became a major political upset when Mr. Tuttle received fifty-four percent of the vote. Then, following national television interviews with fellow New Englanders Jay Leno on the *Tonight Show* and Conan O'Brien on *Late Night*, Mr. Tuttle faced Patrick Leahy, the Democrat's nominee, in the fall election.

Fred lost.

Despite the disappointment this defeat was sort of a relief to Mr. Tuttle, who by this time had other, more important irons in his fire. "I've had the time of my life," he told supporters in his concession speech, "but tomorrow I've got to go dig my potatoes."

He Won't Say

New Hampshire's first-in-the-nation primary is the cherished launch to the every-four-years presidential pageant, and is fashionable among the candidates for its affable air and symbolic votes. Similarly, the primary is embraced by the locals for bringing in lots of cold cash during the otherwise dead of winter.

This periodic incursion is particularly welcomed at the broadcasting complex of WMUR-TV in Manchester. This is a station whose former owner, rumor has it, ran numbers using the "Sermonette" passages and is now owned by the nationwide Hearst-Argyle group, which establishes a periodic base camp for the ABC network and much of the world's media.

Last autumn Enoch Webster drags Henry Foster to a political rally where a candidate is being put on display. As the candidate speaks, his oration goes on too long, and after awhile Enoch's hearing aid starts sounding off and sets to whistling. After the candidate had orated more than Enoch is able to understand, he turns toward Henry.

"What the hell's he talking about?" Enoch wants to know.

"I'm not sure," Henry replies, "He won't say."

Not Even For Fun

The Center Northwood selectmen are known particularly for their prudent ways, the prevailing thought being if you aren't sure about an issue, vote no. After the previous election, though, when the moderator left the ballets in the back of his truck and it rained, they decided to bring in a voting machine sales agent to demonstrate a mechanized approach to voting.

On the morning the sales agent arrived, some of the folks up the Center gathered at the Town House for the presentation. After introducing himself, the agent chooses Walt Palmer to show off the simplicity of this modern voting rig.

"If you flip these levers," the agent shows Walt and everyone, "you'll be voting for individual candidates. Go ahead, give it a try."

Walt steps right up and begins flipping the levers, but just those under the Republican column.

"What he's doing is called 'voting a straight ticket,'" the sales agent tells those gathered, then he shows everyone an easier way to do that. "For example, if he flips the large lever at the top of this column," the agent says, "he will be voting the Democrat slate."

"Gawd, I couldn't do that," says Walt, "not even for fun."

She Ain't Decided

A bunch of the fellahs are down Fred Johnson's garage talking about the election and how things have changed since the ladies got to vote — though most of them admit their wives vote the same way as they do.

"Kinda seems like a waste of paper," Horace Peckham suggests.

"I decided not to vote," admits Henry Foster, who is a bachelor. "I felt like I was just encouraging them."

"Who's your ol' lady voting for?" Roger Hancock asks Horace, whose wife kinda wears the pants in their family.

"Same fellah I'm voting for," Horace admits.

"Who's that going to be?" Henry wants to know.

"She ain't decided yet," Horace says.

I Would Have Been a Democrat

Every now and again, you know, Enoch Webster visits his old Army buddy down Texas. Well, this last trip his buddy invites him to a men's pancake breakfast at a local social club. After everybody sits down, the moderator, catching wise there's a New Englander in attendance, figures on having a little fun.

"I'm doing a little survey this morning, boys," the moderator announces, "Will everybody who's a Democrat please stand up?"

This is at a time when political party lines were still intact, so naturally everyone in the room stands but the lone New Englander. After the Texas boys get seated, the moderator then announces, "If there happens to be a stray Republican got in here, would he mind standing up?" Naturally, the local boys hoot and holler as Enoch gets to his feet.

"Friend," the moderator says to Enoch, "Would you mind telling us what persuaded you to be a Republican?"

"There are two reasons only," Enoch tells him. "First, I'm a born and bred New Englander, and second my father was a Republican before me."

"Those seem like mighty poor reasons," the moderator responds, "Why, supposing your daddy had been a horse thief?"

"Then," Enoch tells him, "I would have been a Democrat."

Still a New Englander

When it comes to politics Roger Hancock is a true independent. "Our patriots died so I could have freedom of choice," he's fond of saying. So what with his wife, Martha, staunchly Republican, and the election drawing near, there have been some rather vigorous discussions around their kitchen table.

Roger drives her nuts criticizing this candidate and that, while she adamantly defends anyone running as a Republican. Or she did until she realized Roger doesn't actually support any candidate.

"You mind telling me something?" she asks him one morning over breakfast, "Since there are only two political parties, and you've already admitted you don't like the Republicans, are you planning to vote Democrat?"

"Golly, I can't do that," he tells her, "I may be independent, but I'm still a New Englander."

9.
The State Store

PROHIBITION WAS THE DIMWITTED DECREE promoted by the Women's Christian Temperance Union and sanctimonious politicians to prohibit the American public from obtaining intoxicating drink. After Prohibition finally collapsed under the weight of its own stupidity, New England became a divided place as the six states had separate opinions as to how to conduct the business of selling liquor legally.

The three northern states chose to sell alcohol through "state stores" with the profit going into the civic purse. The three southern New England states chose to sell spirits through "package stores" — privately-owned stores selling liquor packaged to take away, differentiated from "by the drink" as in bars — and charging a state liquor tax. The result in the southern three states is only political cronies got liquor licenses, and the public is forced to pay *both* the store's profit and the state tax. Needless to say, liquor is cheaper in northern New England.

☛ Perhaps the most influential of all New England political dynasties is that of the Kennedys. And perhaps the singly most influential American power broker in the twentieth century was Joseph P. Kennedy, Sr. of Boston.

Born in 1888, Mr. Kennedy became a big shot among Massachusetts Democrats after he married Rose Fitzgerald — arguably the real power behind the broker whose father was Boston's notorious mayor Honey Fitz, a power broker in a day when "Irish politician" meant patronage and political favors. Right off, Rose and Joe began begetting a flock of children to carry on the Kennedy name.

Where there's power there's usually money, lots of it. And Mr. Kennedy obtained much from brokering a vast portfolio of stocks. But to obtain a vast portfolio of stocks, first he had to come up with the initial loot to pay for it — which is where Prohibition comes in. Prohibition was supposed to end the distribution of alcohol in America, what it actually accomplished was to throw down the welcome mat to organized crime, and among the great crime coalitions was the Irish mob of Boston.

Mr. Kennedy finagled a deal where he obtained a U.S. government license to import alcohol from distillers in Great Britain, supposedly for medical purposes. At the close of Prohibition Mr. Kennedy was by then sitting on a vast hoard of legal hooch, which he promptly leveraged into a vast heap of cash and stocks.

He then brokered this vast wealth into Democratic political favors, finally buying himself the ambassadorship to Great Britain, where he made an embarrassing ass of himself. Which doesn't matter in politics. Consequently, his offspring, grandchildren, and great grandchildren, now have the cash and clout to carry on forevermore the influence of the Kennedy name.

Visiting Grandfather

Henry Foster is over to the State Store fetching a jug of Barbados rum. Since Henry's a teetotaler, Sam Mason, the store's manager, isn't quite sure why.

"Oh, this ain't for me," Henry tells him, "It's for my old man."

"How's he doing?" Sam asks.

"I just took him up Rumford Falls to see his father," Henry says, "Pa likes to go see Grandfather on his birthday."

"Then his dad's still kickin'?" Sam asks.

"Grandfather just turned a hundred and one," Henry replies, "So we're going along all right, when Pa reaches in and comes up with a jug of Barbados rum. So as we're trundling along, Pa every now and again he takes himself a snort.

"Well sir, by the time we get down Rumford Falls, he's feeling kinda jolly, eyeballs sticking right out. When Grandfather sees us, he comes out on a trot and sides up. 'You got a snort for me?' he wants to know. 'I might find you a snort,' I say, 'but remember your age.'

"Well, Grandfather is built sot of peculiar. His skin's gone down under his chin all floppy — it kinda reminds you of a gobbler turkey. So I pass him the jug, and Grandfather, he tips it back and fills that sack solid full, swallows it down, and starts a-coughing and a-wheezing, and after a spell he catches his breath and says, 'Gawd, that's good.'

"About that time the telephone rings, and Grandfather, he grabs it. It's his fiancé. Seems he's getting married again."

"What's he want to get married for at his age?" Sam asks.

"Gawd, he don't want to," Henry replies, "He's got to."

The Toilet Key

Fred Johnson was down to Boston, and while he was there he steps into one of those bars. Fred's been a drinking man all his life, but this is the first time he's ever tried it out in one of those bars.

Well sir, he steps up and asks for a beer. The place has quite a selection, which kinda throws Fred a mite since we only have Frank Jones Ale, Narragansett Lager, and a couple other kinds up here. The barkeeper finally gives him a bottle of Harvard Green Label Lager, which Fred orders because it sounds like an intelligent pick.

He's sitting there nursing the beer when a fellah comes in, has a drink, then after a spell says something to the bartender. The bartender hands the fellah something that looks like it might be a key, and he goes out. In a few minutes he comes back and turns in the key. Fred just sits there watching as this happens two or three times as other fellahs come and go.

"What's that key you're giving them fellahs?" Fred finally asks the bartender.

"Oh, that's just the toilet key," the bartender tells him, "You need to use it?"

"No, not yet anyway," Fred replies. He ponders this a while before he says, "You keep that locked up, do you?"

"Boss's orders," says the bartender, "You want to use it?"

"I got no use for it," Fred replies, "but I can't figure out why in the world you'd want to lock that place up. Where I come from out back of the store, Bill Peterson has a privy there that anybody can use. He's never thought to lock it up; matter of fact the last couple of years there hasn't even been a door on it, but so far as I know, nobody's ever stolen any manure out of it."

Barbados Rum

"I tied one on good t'other night — the demon rum," Fred Johnson's admitting.

Since there's a nor'easter howling and not much else doing, a bunch of fellahs are hanging out over to Fred's garage. "When I came through the kitchen door," Fred continues, "My old lady, she just took that frying pan and whacked me over my head."

"Gawd, she could've killed you," Horace Peckham sympathizes, having gone down that same trail with his own wife.

"I don't know about that," Fred says, "but it did startle me some."

"I ain't tasted rum in twenty-five years," Walt Palmer chimes in, "and I recall like t'was yesterday the time I took me that last drink."

"In them days I built boats, and I built coffins, too," Walt continues, "As a matter of fact, I built most of the coffins them folks up to the churchyard's buried in. I recollect the weather was just like today, all cold and raw, and I'd just built a catboat for Dr. Kenny.

"Charley Snow comes down and says he needs a coffin by Thursday. I tell him it's rather short notice, and he says he knows it is, but he'd brought with him a jug of Barbados rum to keep me going. I tell him I'll do my best, and I didn't spare myself none, nor did I spare any of that rum.

"Come Thursday, Charley drives down in the morning, and I tell him I'd just finished. So, I take him down to my boatshed, and I open the door, but I notice Charley kind of started some. Then I look in, and there she sets and godfrey if she doesn't have a rudder and a centerboard on her."

Judgment Day

Jeremiah Coates was picked up last night for being underage and intoxicated in public. Seems his half-brother, Junior, had fetched him a bottle from the State Store, and now he's standing there in front of Judge Pratt.

"Well, young fellah," the judge says, "The law says I've got to fine you five dollars."

"You always do everything you're told?" Jeremiah answers back.

"Just pay the fine, and you can go," says Judge Pratt, who's tired of seeing Jeremiah coming into court, which happens on a somewhat regular basis.

"Am I getting something to show for this?" Jeremiah questions the judge.

"You got a hangover, don't you?" the judge replies.

"I mean, one of them papers," Jeremiah persists.

"A receipt, they call it," the judge says.

"Yeah, a receipt," Jeremiah says, "You gotta give me one of them receipts."

"The clerk will write one out for you," the judge informs him, "Why, don't you trust us?"

"You're old and you're gonna die," Jeremiah tells him, "and someday I'll get old like you. That's right, ain't it judge?"

"I suppose it is," he replies.

"And after I'm gathered," Jeremiah says, "I'll be standing before the Lord, just like I'm standing here now. Ain't that right?"

"That's my understanding," says the judge.

"And he's probably gonna ask if I've been in trouble like you did," Jeremiah says, "and I'll have to admit I got drunk and arrested. Then the Lord's gonna want to know if I was fined, and I'll tell him I was. So when he asks me if I paid the fine, I don't want him hunting all over hell looking for you."

The Beer Samples

Tom Lillibridge and Matt Conley are off-loading their catches over to Fish's Dock when they get to talking about beer, and particularly which one's the best. After debating this back and forth, Tom favoring Frank Jones Ale to Matt's Narragansett Lager, Walt Palmer finally comes up with what they agree is a mighty fine idea.

"I should think the only fair-minded way to resolve this," Walt suggests, "is to send samples of both to one of them laboratories and get their decision."

Well, none of them have a clue how to find a laboratory until Walt remembers he'd given a specimen to Dr. Kenny, who'd sent it out to a laboratory in Boston. With that in mind, Tom and Matt are all set to drive up Dr. Kenny's, when Walt has one further recommendation.

"You know the saying, 'Old soldiers never die, they just fade away?'" he asks.

"Yessah," Tom replies.

"Well boys, there's another saying," he tells them, "'Old fishermen never die, they just smell that way.'"

So after taking the hint and bathing, Tom and Matt run up to Dr. Kenny's office in Center Northwood. The doctor has them pour their two samples into a couple of sterilized jars, and then he mails them off to the laboratory.

After the report arrives, Dr. Kenny has Tom and Matt back in to read the results. Opening the envelope, Dr. Kenny reads aloud, "Gentlemen, thank you for submitting your specimens, however we must inform you that due to the high level of alcohol, we advise you to adopt a strict regimen of temperance and self-discipline."

Three Kinds of Turd

Joe Hancock takes the Boston & Maine train down Boston, where he decides to stay at the Hotel Statler. After he checks in, he goes over to the elevator.

"Would you mind taking me to the fourth floor?" he says to the elevator operator, "That's if it don't take you out of your way."

He gets up there and washes up a mite, then he figures he'd like to get a drink someplace. Joe ambles back downstairs again, where he finds a cocktail lounge right there off the lobby.

"I think I should like to have me a drink of gin," he tells the bartender. Well, that bartender kinda senses this fellah's from upcountry, so he thought he might have a little fun.

"We have three kinds of gin here," the bartender tells him — which throws Joe off a mite. Back home in Center Northwood, any gin he's had came from that still Bill Peterson has set up in the shed out behind his store.

"What you got?" Joe inquires.

"Well, we have some Nitro Gin, some Hydro Gin, and we have some Oxy Gin," the bartender tells him, "So which kind would you like?"

Joe's no fool, and he recalls out behind Bill Peterson's store, there's also an outhouse.

"So you got three kinds of gin, do you?" Joe says, "Where I come from we have three kinds of turd — we got Mus Turd, we got Cus Turd, and now by Gawd, we got you. Now fetch me a drink."

10.
Horses & Horseless Carriages

IN 1813 WHEELWRIGHT LEWIS DOWNING at the age of 21 traveled from his home in Lexington, Massachusetts up to Concord, New Hampshire to see his fiancé Lucy Wheelock, and he stayed there, starting a "waggon" business in 1816.

By 1825 Concord had become the hub of northern New England's stage transportation, and in 1828 Mr. Downing was joined by master coachbuilder J. Stephen Abbot, and together they created the first of fourteen models of their famed Concord Coach.

The body of each coach was curved for strength, reinforced with iron bands, and rested on unique three-inch oxen leather "thorough braces" which acted like a hammock that gently swayed the cab, preventing injury to the horses. Mark Twain described them as "an imposing cradle on wheels."

The interior was upholstered in leather and damask cloth, and each balanced wheel was made of seasoned white oak with handmade spokes so carefully fitted to the rim and hub it was difficult to detect where they joined.

The company was hereafter known as Abbott-Downing, a name that became to coaches what Cadillac would later become to motorcars. The Abbott-Downing Concord Coach was used by both Overland Trail Stage Route and Wells Fargo & Company, making them the "wheels that crossed America" opening the West.

☛ At the time of these stories, however, the carriage of choice was Henry Ford's self-propelled, gasoline powered Model T automobile, which was available in any color "so long as it's black."

Although not the first workhorse to gallop under manufactured horsepower, the "tin Lizzie", as they were known, was the first car to be built on a moving assembly line. Over fifteen million Model T cars and trucks were manufactured from 1908 to 1927, and by 1918 half of the vehicles in the United States were Model T's, making the Ford Motor Company the largest automobile manufacturer in the world.

Because they were inexpensive and easy to handle on rough roads, Model T's became prevalent in New England cities and towns. Before long these tin Lizzies were like cherished family members with folks assigning personalities to their T's, cussedness being the general trait.

As Model T's and other automobiles proliferated on downtown streets, Boston became the first municipality in the nation to install traffic signals, and consequently the first with drivers running red lights for which they're still infamous. Then came Boston's unique combination red and yellow signal, an area peculiarity indicating pedestrians crossing, but which mostly mystifies tourists and other visitors from "away."

Dead Air Pocket

Some of the fellahs are gathered at the counter in Lew Cottrell's Minuteman Diner. Lew's talking, hollering from the kitchen actually, about a Ford Model T car he'd purchased used up Center Northwood.

"You heard about the Liz I bought?" he shouts.

"The one you pinched from that old lady?" Matt Conley laughs.

"She never used it but to go to church," Lew says, "The upholstery is all good, but the mud pan was a mite loose. So I hooked it up, and in no time at all she was running just as smooth as smelt."

"She's a honey," Charley Snow agrees.

"That old Liz can jump puddles as quick as a cat," Lew shouts, "but when I started up North Road, she started going jump, jump, jump like a rabbit. So I shifted her, then she started chattering like a squirrel on a wall."

"It wasn't the mud pan?" Ann Champlin, the waitress, chimes in.

"The pan was alright and everything," Lew continues, "but I didn't know if we'd get back to the Center or not. When we did, I was waiting around Fred Johnson's garage, and one of them city chauffeurs pulls up to the filling pump."

"He was up for a funeral," Charley comments.

"So I told him about my difficulties with Liz," Lew says, "and you know what that chauffeur told me? He said I must have hit one of them dead air pockets."

Don't Give a Damn

Josiah Coates finds an old busted hay wagon out in the woods, so he fetches Larry, that ancient draft horse of his, and pulls that wagon out onto North Road and heads down toward where his trailer sets — but things aren't going too good. About then his youngest son, Jeremiah, comes walking up.

"Larry keeps running into stuff," Jeremiah comments.

"Nothing wrong with that horse," Josiah replies.

"He's blind," Jeremiah states.

"He ain't blind," Josiah says, "Larry just don't give a damn."

Which Way To Rumford Falls?

In the early part of the twentieth century, there began to appear what automobile dealers today call "previously owned vehicles" but were referred to locally as "flivvers". As a matter of fact, Merriam-

Webster, the distinguished New England dictionary publisher, traces this word to the year 1910.

Junior Coates is standing on the porch of Bill Peterson's Country Store sucking on a bottle of Moxie when a flivver approaches and stops out front.

"Which way to Rumford Falls?" the driver shouts.

"Well, you could go this way a spell," Junior tells him, pointing toward North Road up Granite Mountain, "and when you get to the split in the road, you could go another six or eight miles, then turn onto...

"No, you better stay on this road a couple of miles or so, make a right turn where the old barn with Hurd's Feed & Grain painted on it used to be, and follow that about five miles more or less to...

"Or you can follow the notch down to the Coast Road, and take a left when you see the Socony filling station, or whatever it's called now, pass the diner and stay on that road 'til you come to...

"Rumford Falls?" Junior says, "Come to think of it, you can't get there from here."

Tall Tale

"One time I was down Wood River fly fishing," Horace Peckham tells the fellahs gathered around Fred Johnson's garage, "When a bear comes up and starts chasing me. Well sir, he was right on my tail when I spotted a tree branch and took a leap for it."

"One of them oaks?" Fred asks, just to keep the story going.

"I think it was an elm," Horace says, "No matter, the branch broke, and I fell to the ground.

"He getcha?" Walt Palmer asks.

"Fortunately, that old bear was running by so fast," Horace says, "That by the time he saw me and got rethreaded, I was running the opposite way."

"And you had a considerable lead on him, too," Matt Conley adds.

"Of course," Horace replies, "Well sir, that bear chased me from August to November, when I finally got an idea and led that old bear out over Arrow Lake."

"Arrow Lake's not frozen in November," Henry Foster interrupts.

"It is in this story," Horace continues, "but when we got out over the middle where the lake is deep and the ice is thin, that old bear just broke through and drowned."

"So, the story's not the only thing that's all wet," Fred remarks.

Tourists

Upcountry between the mountains are ravines the locals call notches, and each spring these notches begin to fill up with rain, mud, blackflies, and tourists.

"A tourist fellah comes by the docks t'other day," Tom Lillibridge is saying. Tom's sitting about with the other fellahs up to Lew Cottrell's Minuteman Diner. "And this tourist remarks there's a lot of strange people around here. 'Yes there are,' I tell him, 'but you'll all be gone come September.'"

"I run into an awful fracas t'other morning," Lew states, "I got that old T, you know. I bought it figuring I'd get to drive it some before the tourists come around. There's getting to be an awful pile of them these days. Anyway, I was climbing up the notch — she stalls out a wicked lot up there — and I see one of those summer fellahs, a New York car, and he comes right along and whizzes by. Well sir, I just thought that old flivver of mine had stalled out again, so I jumped out, and damn if she didn't run me over."

"Which explains the bandages," Tom observes.

"Scratched me up something wicked," Lew says.

Horse Startin'

Walt Palmer is of the old school and claims he prefers getting about with a horse and wagon. Since Walt's kinda tightfisted, most of us pretty much figure he's just too cheap to buy a truck.

Walt's down Center Northwood, and he's kinda in a hurry. He gets his horse hitched up to the wagon, and he starts along pretty good until he gets up Old Notch Road, and the horse quits on him. He doesn't know what happened, maybe a bit of newspaper or something blew across the road and scared her.

"Come on Harriet," he says, "Come on and get a-going."

Well, that horse just stood there, so Walt removes the whip from the whip socket and whacks her some on the rump, but that horse just won't budge. Finally after a spell of not making any progress, Walt starts beating that horse from Beersheba to be damned, but there she stands. He'd pretty much given up, when down the road comes Junior Coates.

"Having a little horse trouble, Mr. Palmer?" Junior asks.

"Yes I am, Junior," says Walt, "I've thumped this beast for fifteen, twenty minutes, but she's kinda froze up on me."

"You know, Mr. Palmer," Junior replies, "I just happen to have a little tin of turpentine in my pocket, and I believe that just might get this horse started."

"I'd certainly appreciate if you could help me," says Walt.

"You go around the backend of that horse and lift her tail up," says Junior, "and I'll just put a drop or two of this where I think it will do the most good."

Well sir, he did, and that horse's head shot right up, and she lit off through that notch — why you couldn't see the wagon or the horse for all the dust.

"I don't believe I've ever seen a better job of horse starting," Walt tells him, "but there's just one thing."

"What's that, Mr. Palmer?" Junior asks.

"I was hoping to get home myself, and besides that I've got to catch that horse," Walt says, "I don't presume you'd have a drop or two more of that turpentine, would you?"

Kick Startin'

Junior Coates's wife, Lulu, she's a lot like Junior. The fact is they're both as numb as hake. After all these years of using a horse and wagon to haul about in, Junior finally takes some of that money he'd earned felling trees for the Northwood Paper Company, and he buys a used truck — an excessively used Model T with a flat bed made of oak planks from up the sawmill.

Well sir, that truck ran slick as ice the day he bought it from that fellah down Rumford Falls, but when he got it back up Granite Mountain it started running wicked peculiar and has ever since. In fact in order to get it going on a cold morning, Junior has to get it rolling down North Road before he can pop the clutch and kick it into gear.

And that's where that wife of his comes in. Junior needs that old truck rolling at about thirty-five, so as Lulu does the pushing, Junior sits in the driver's seat ready to pop the clutch. And it all works pretty good, too — except that first time.

That first time, after he explains to Lulu that she has to get the truck going thirty-five, Junior waits for her to start pushing. After he'd been sitting a spell and the truck's not budging, he looks in the rearview mirror and godfrey mighty here comes Lulu running right toward him at a full thirty-five mile-an-hour clip.

Whoa

Walt Palmer comes along as Junior Coates is hauling logs on Granite Mountain. Junior's borrowed Larry, his old man's ancient draft horse, but he keeps stopping all the time.

"You'll never get finished this way," Walt says.

"This old horse is hard of hearing," Junior replies.

"I don't see what that's got to do with it," Walt says to him.

"He stops to listen," Junior tells him, "Larry's just afraid I'll say 'whoa', and he won't hear me."

The Richfield Sign

A sales agent from the Richfield Oil Company drops by Fred Johnson's garage. Fred is working under a truck on the lift at the time.

"We're going to have to replace that sign out front", the agent tells Fred, who doesn't give a damn what Richfield does with its sign. It's one of those enameled metal signs on a post that's lit on both sides by spotlights stuck out on pipes. What the company wants to do is replace it with one of those modern signs that's illuminated from inside.

Well as I say, Fred doesn't care until the agent mentions the company expects Fred to pay for the new sign. From there the conversation slides downhill with the agent insisting and Fred telling him to go fry ice.

After a spell of disagreeing back and forth, Fred, without saying a word, goes outside, jumps into his wrecker parked out back, and drives around front. He attaches the winch cable to the signpost, hops back into his wrecker, and yanks that sign, post and all, right out of the ground. He hauls it around back and drops it over where he keeps the junk cars. The Richfield agent is just standing there watching through the windows. Finally, after parking the wrecker in the same spot it was before, Fred comes back inside.

"Ain't nobody around here don't already know I sell gas," Fred tells him, "I don't need no goddam sign."

Don't Look Too Good

Tony Briggs, Matt Conley's hired man, thinks he'd like to try his hand at the draft horse competition come the next County Agricultural Fair. Not wise to matters of horse-trading, however, Tony goes up to Josiah Coates, who, you know, isn't too accurate regarding the truth. Since Josiah stretches a blanket pretty good, he shows Tony his ancient draft horse, Larry.

"Got to tell you, Larry don't look too good," Josiah admits.

"I don't care about that," Tony says, "Just so long as he's a rugged critter."

So they settle on a price, and Tony takes that old horse down to Matt's place, where he soon learns that Larry keeps running into things. In a week's time Tony's back up to Josiah's with the horse wanting his money back.

"I ain't giving you a cent," Josiah tells him.

"This horse you sold me is stone blind!" Tony contends.

"Gawd," Josiah says, "Didn't I tell you Larry don't look too good?"

One Sick Hog

"Joe and I were blasting some stumps out back," Roger Hancock tells the fellahs gathered around Fred Johnson's garage, "then I put the left over dynamite in the barn and forgot about it. Well, you remember that old hog of mine?"

"We mostly feed it scraps and stuff," says Joe, Roger's older boy.

"It will eat anything," Roger continues, "anything we set before it. Well, it wandered into the barn t'other afternoon and got into that bag of dynamite."

"That was when I was coming back from the Center," Joe says.

"That hog must have got disoriented by the dynamite," Roger says, "and it steps right out in front of Joe's truck."

"Baaaam!" Joe says, "I thought I was a goner."

"Blew out some windows in the barn," Roger tells them.

"Dented the truck something wicked," Joe adds.

"And for a week now we've been nursing one mighty sick hog," says Roger.

That's Once

Not too many folks remember that Josiah Coates was married once, and they had quite a wedding up to the Congregational Meeting House. Josiah had brought his horse and wagon down, so after the reception, he loads in his bride, and with Josiah sitting right up there close to her, they start back up Granite Mountain.

Josiah, he's not much of a hand at talking. After they'd gone through the covered bridge and headed up North Road, which gets mighty rough in places, that old horse stumbles.

"That's once," says Josiah.

This is the first time he's said a word since setting off from the church. They continue along a piece, when that horse stumbles again.

"That's twice," says Josiah.

They go along another mile or two, and that old horse stumbles again, but this time Josiah doesn't say a word. He just reigns back, and jumps out of the wagon. Josiah walks around back, hauls out his shotgun, draws off two or three feet from that horse, and drops it dead right there in the shafts. Well, that young bride of his, she just fusses up something wicked. "That's a terrible thing you did," she whimpers right there in the middle of the road. "And he was a nice old horse, too!"

"That's once," Josiah says.

In The Bushes

The fellahs were sitting around Fred Johnson's garage t'other day talking about this, that and the other when they started talking about Model T's and how one time most everyone around here had one.

"I have one of the best T's they is," Spud Carpenter's saying, "One thing about her, though, she won't run up through the notch without boiling over, not unless I stop and water her up at that spring half way.

"One warm evening last spring Isabelle and I thought we'd drive up to the Center, so we get the old T a-shuttering, and we start the run up Old Notch Road. We come to that spring, and I know I have to water her up, or she'll boil over. I always keep a bucket in the back seat, so I pull up to that spring, get out the bucket, go fill it up, and turn that bucket in. She's already steaming some, and that old T, she drinks it right down like she's dried up good.

"So I go back over to that spring, fill the bucket again, and turn that second load in. All the while Isabelle is just sitting there watching. This time the old T only takes in about a quarter of it and slops over, so where's there's no other machines in sight, no signs of life or nothing like that, I kinda slosh that bucket off into the bushes.

"Soon as I sloshed it, though, that young Coates boy, Jeremiah, sticks his head up from them bushes. I'd wetted him down something awful, not that I had a mind to, of course, but he commences to swear something wicked. He calls me an ornery old so and so, and things I can't even repeat here.

"So, after he slows down a mite, I look him straight in the eyes. 'That ain't no way to talk, you know,' I say to him, 'Can't you see I got a lady in the car?'"

"And you know what he says to me?" Spud says, "'Whatdaya think I got here in the bushes, a duck?'"

Wives

As usual the fellah's are sitting around Fred Johnson's garage shooting the breeze when they fetch up on the subject of wives.

"Mary Ann takes courses up to the State College," Matt Conley is saying, "and now she's talking my ears off on most any subject."

"That's nothing," Horace Peckham chimes in, "Eileen, she talks for hours on end, and she don't hardly need a subject."

Horse Trading

You remember Josiah Coates tried to pass off his deaf, blind, and busted down old draft horse, Larry, on Tony Briggs, but he didn't get away with it. Well, Larry finally died this morning, and since Josiah doesn't know how to dispose of the remains without it entailing a whole lot of work, he hatches up a scheme to get his son, Junior, to do it.

You remember also, there's the saying, "the apple doesn't fall far from the tree?" Well sir, it just might be so.

"I know you got that riding horse over here," Josiah declares. Junior's none too sharp, but he knows damn well for his old man to walk all the way over to his cabin across the mountain, there must be a skunk in the woods.

"What do you want with that horse of mine?" Junior wants to know.

"What you really need is that draft horse of mine," Josiah replies.

"Yeah?" Junior queries.

"I thought you might wanna trade," says Josiah.

"What terms?" Junior asks.

"Even," Josiah replies.

"Done," says Junior, and they shake hands on it.

"There's something I gotta tell you," Josiah says, "That old horse, he died this morning."

"And there's something you ought to know," Junior replies, "I buried that horse of mine last week."

A double-ender fishing schooner sorting out Cod Point reef.

11.
Nor'easters & Sou'westers

NEW ENGLAND SETS AT THE CONVERGENCE of several wind and water currents that influence atmospheric conditions across the region, causing some of the harshest weather patterns on the planet. Nonetheless, some of the nation's mildest water temperatures lay along the south shore of Cape Cod, which embraces the northern flow of the tropical Gulf Stream. What's more, come summer when the winds of the transcontinental Jet Stream hug the northern states, New England then undergoes alternating wind patterns of Caribbean steam and Canadian cool.

Despite the rigors of the region's hodgepodge weather, there are certain New Englanders who just won't be intimidated by it. Up on Boston Harbor, blocked from the warming Gulf Stream by Cape Cod, is the James Michael Curley Community Center, self-named by the city's former mayor and a gift to his loyal constituents in this heavily Irish district of the city. Popularly known as the L Street Bathhouse, this bathing and athletic club is home to South Boston's famed "L Street Brownies", a society of about seventy-five men and women so named for their perpetual tans from sunbathing and swimming the year 'round, oftentimes defying shoreline ice to do it.

The L Street Brownies trace their origins to 1865, but it wasn't until 1902 that the group formally incorporated and started gaining fame when they initiated their invigorating New Year's Day "polar bear" dips for anyone who'd show up. Today about five-hundred hearty and fool-hearty souls come to frolic in the near-freezing harbor waters — many in costumes, such as one Elvis, two Santa Clauses, and a Superman, who got cold feet and only went in up to his ankles.

☞ On the morning of April 11, 1934, just two years after the Mount Washington Observatory had been built in New Hampshire, the crew was enjoying a clear view of the North Atlantic Ocean from the 6288-foot summit, some seventy miles from the coast. This view, however, rapidly surrendered to increasing clouds caused by a convergence of a weak storm system approaching over the Great Lakes to the west, a second approaching storm off the North Carolina coast to the south, and a huge ridge of high pressure stalled over the Maritime Provinces to the east.

Fog began obscuring the summit. As high pressure built to the northeast, and low pressure approached in the west, an intense pressure gradient caused wind to quickly blast from the high pressure to the low-pressure. Soon rime ice of up to a foot deep encrusted the Observatory as winds increased to 136 miles per hour, well over hurricane strength.

The following morning ice had obscured the specially heated anemometer so much that Wendell Stephenson, a crew member, suited up and taking a wooden bat, worked his way through the wind blasts to free the equipment. Inside the Observatory, the crew was verifying gusts of 150 miles per hour — from the *southeast*, a very rare occurrence. By noon the wind was registering 229 miles per hour, then at 1:21 P.M. it gusted to 231 miles per hour.

Sal Pagliuca, another crew member, entered into the log that day, "'Will they believe it?' was our first thought. I felt then the full responsibility of that startling measurement. Was my timing correct? Was the method OK? Was the calibration curve right? Was the stop watch accurate?"

Although the storm lasted just a day, the equipment needed to be run through tests. It was then that the highest surface wind measured anywhere on earth was confirmed by the National Weather Bureau for April 12, 1934 at Mount Washington, New Hampshire. This "World's Record Wind" is a record that still stands today.

Mud Time

It's been wicked snowy followed by a wet spell, and it's setting mud so much up on Moose Head Trail, a guy can get cross-threaded if he's not wearing snowshoes. One afternoon Horace Peckham is down to Fred Johnson's garage, and he's talking about just how muddy it's gotten up his way.

"I went out to my mailbox," he's saying, "and I spot something up there right in the middle of the road, and it's kinda working its way toward me. At first I thought it might be a cat or something, but there wasn't any tail on it I could see."

"It might have been one of them bobtail cats," Henry Foster suggests, "but there ain't no bobtail cats in town, I know about."

"Well, that thing keeps a-working its way toward me," Horace says, "so I wonder if it might not be a woodchuck."

"You know darned well woodchucks don't hang in the middle of the road like that," Fred says.

"That's right, so by the time the thing's worked its way up close," Horace continues, "I see it's a brown hat, so I pick it up, and under it is Junior Coates's head, his nose sticking right out over the mud, his mouth just barely clearing."

"Golly," says Joe Hancock, who's been hanging around Fred's a half hour just looking to buy gasoline.

"I lean over good so Junior can hear me," Horace says, "'Kinda muddy walking, ain't it, Junior?' 'Oh, I ain't afoot, Mr. Peckham', Junior tells me, 'I'm a-horse back.'"

Get Any Frost?

After doing chores, Spud Carpenter makes the run over Bill Peterson's Country Store in Center Northwood. It's chilly this morning, wicked chilly, but the sun is strong as he drives down.

"You get any frost up your place?" Bill asks, after Spud settles into the warmth of the potbelly woodstove.

"When I got up, I always get up early, you know," Spud tells him, "Pa and Ma always taught us boys to get up in the morning. There ain't a lay-in-bed among us.

"Well, I got up and headed downstairs. Now, them stairs of mine have a nice twelve-inch tread with about a six-inch riser, and the tread is made of solid oak. There ain't no ruts in the middle of them treads, and they are nice and easy to go down. You're not going to have any fuss like you do on them tall stairs, no sir. Now, that banister of mine is red cherry, and there at the bottom is a post of curly ash. I'll tell you, there ain't nothing so pretty first thing in the morning as that combination of red cherry and curly ash.

"As I say, I went downstairs to my parlor. Now that parlor of mine has one of them kerosene oil heaters. I light that heater up when I come in from my evening chores, and the next morning that room's just as warm as toast, I'll tell you. Now, in my parlor I have me a walnut sofa and two chairs all upholstered in red plush, and it's mighty pretty, I'll say. And next to the sofa I have me a standing lamp with a globe that's a cream color. It's mighty nice coming in at night and stretching out on that sofa. On Thursday evenings when *The Northwood Independent* comes out, it's about nine, nine-thirty before I get up and go to bed.

"Then I went out through my dining room with the wainscoting. A dining room just ain't a dining room without wainscoting, I'll tell you, and the wainscoting in my dining room is butternut wood. Why, it just makes you hungry looking at it.

"Isabelle, she was already down the kitchen at the cookstove. Now, I use maple and birch in my cookstove, and I keep a cord in the shed. The rest of it is up on the woodlot seasoning. So, I went through the shed to the outhouse.

"I used boxwood in my privy. Why, there ain't nothing so comfortable in the entire world than boxwood, all velvety and smooth, you know. Now, you've got to face an outhouse quartering into the wind, and the prevailing wind up our way is sou'west, so my privy faces just a mite east of south. This makes a big difference how the wind comes through them holes, I'll say.

"Then, I went out to the barn to fetch my dog, Liberty. Now, Libby, I'll tell you, is the best cow dog there's ever been raised. So Libby and me, we start our way out the runway. I used galvanized fencing with cedar posts all around my pasture. You use any other posts, and they start to rot before you sink them in the ground, but with cedar you have a fence.

"So Libby and me, we head toward the runway gate, and when we got out there, I just happened to look down and you know, there on the ground was just a small mite of frost."

Leakin' Roof

I suppose it's not right calling a fellah stupid, but those Coates boys are bent way over. It's driving rain as Junior Coates works his way across a dank Granite Mountain to that rickety trailer his old man, Josiah, calls home. Junior has to go over every afternoon to call in the cows, since they pretty much ignore Josiah. Junior bangs on the trailer door.

"Go away," Josiah hollers from inside.

"It's me," Junior shouts back, after which the door swings open allowing Junior to see empty food tins scattered about catching rainwater pouring through the ceiling.

"Roof leaking?" Junior asks.

"It's raining," his old man tells him.

"Why don't you fix it?" Junior wants to know.

"'Cause it's raining," Josiah replies.

"Fix it when it ain't raining," Junior suggests.

"Then it ain't leaking," Josiah says.

Don't Even Know It

Edna Phelps and Enoch Webster are among the oldest citizens in town, and they're both doing pretty well, aside from failing eyesight, pigheadedness, and the other lapses common to old age.

There'd been a nor'east blow and fierce rain for nearly a week solid, so when the weather finally breaks one sunny morning, Edna decides to take a drive over Snug Harbour to look around, and to stop at Whaler's Inn for coffee and a cranberry muffin. She parks her car at the far end of the gravel parking area in order to give herself a distance to stroll, and when she does she notices a fellah she thinks might be Enoch.

"Good morning," Edna shouts, "and how are you this fine day?"

"None of your business," the fellah replies.

"Now Enoch, that's no way to talk," she scolds.

"I'm not Enoch," the fellah says, "I don't even know an Enoch."

"Aren't you Enoch Webster?" Edna asks.

"I already told you I'm not," the fellah insists.

"You look like him," Edna persists.

"Well, I'm not him," the fellah repeats.

"You are, too, Enoch Webster," Edna asserts.

"I tell you, I'm not," the fellah pleads.

"You're Enoch Webster," declares Edna, "and you don't even know it."

You Stuck?

One afternoon as an unexpected winter storm settles over Center Northwood and the surrounding mountains, Roger Hancock is running up the notch toward Sugar Hill, trying to beat the blizzard home. He makes the turn onto the dirt foothill road okay and gets past the covered bridge, when his truck does a doughnut on some snow-covered ice and the right rear wheel slides into the brook.

Having no choice, Roger trudges back in the snow, through the bridge to the nearby grist mill to call home.

"Yes?" his wife answers.

"That you, Martha?" he asks.

"Of course it's me," Martha confirms.

"How's everything?" he asks.

"You're stuck, aren't you?" Martha inquires.

"If I were going someplace, I suppose I'd be," he replies.

The Town Line

The state Public Works Department sent an engineer up Granite Mountain to survey the curve on North Road. After all these years, they've finally decided it's too dangerous, particularly during harsh winter conditions, so they're straightening it out.

When he finishes the survey, though, the state engineer also discovers the town line's off by an eighth of a mile. About then Josiah Coates comes huffing and puffing along on that rusty old bicycle of his.

"What you doing on my property?" Josiah demands to know.

"This is state land," the engineer informs him.

"I live here," Josiah says, not acknowledging he's actually a squatter.

"So that's your trailer back there," the engineer asks.

"What if it is?" Josiah demands.

"Just that all this time we thought this was Rumford Falls," the engineer tells him, "but it turns out your trailer's actually setting in Center Northwood."

"Good," says Josiah, "I don't think I could take another Rumford Falls winter."

More Bull

Up to Fred Johnson's Richfield filling station and garage there's a sign hanging there that appropriately reads:

> **Cows may come and cows may go, but the BULL in this place goes on forever!**

Well sir, some of the fellahs are up to Fred's swapping lies when that German, the summer visitor, comes in.

"That horse of yours," Enoch Webster says to the fellah, "He got any speed in him?"

"One time I got caught in a thunder storm up there," the German brags, "My horse is so fast, I never felt a drop."

"Them storms come up quick o'er Granite Mountain," Henry Foster confirms.

"My dog, though," the German continues, "He was trailing behind and had to swim the distance."

"All that rain we're having," Henry adds, "it's raising a wicked crop of mosquitoes."

"There's so many mosquitoes up my way, they ate my horse," Enoch says, "By the time I got out there, they were tossing horseshoes to see who'd get me."

"The weather's sure been rough this year," Henry agrees.

"They say we got but two seasons," Fred replies, "winter and July."

"I was in that dog sled race last winter," Joe Hancock says, when a blizzard comes up over that mountain."

"Wicked awful," Henry confirms.

"Damn right it was," Joe says, "Got lost and had to eat one of my dogs. Rummaged through my kit half a day before I found the mustard."

12.
The Hub Of the Universe

UPON THE COMPLETION of the gold-domed Massachusetts State House high upon Beacon Hill, Boston physician and writer Dr. Oliver Wendel Holmes, Sr., father of Supreme Court Justice Holmes, remarked the place would become "the hub of the solar system." Taking this to be scholarly opinion, Bostonians soon concluded their city, therefore, must be "the hub of the universe."

Founded in 1630, Boston today is a compact cosmopolitan city of over 590,000, and with its equally erudite neighboring cities and towns is home to some 175,000 students attending thirty-four colleges and universities. Additionally, the city is home to the Museum of Fine Arts, Boston Symphony, Boston Ballet, John Fitzgerald Kennedy Presidential Library, Museum of Science, Red Sox, Celtics, Bruins, Cheers, and other institutions of learning and popular culture.

Since our's is the only known humanity in the universe, and inasmuch as the cultural centers of antiquity have each had their day, it seems perfectly fitting and honorable for Boston to seize stewardship of civilization and declare itself the hub of universal sophistication and culture. So much for Yankee reserve.

☛ The foundation of culture and learning in America was laid with the establishment of Harvard College in 1636. The foundation began to crack, however, with the creation of the Hasty Pudding Society by twenty-one Harvard students in 1795.

The stated mission of this organization named for a cornmeal porridge was "to cultivate the social affections and cherish the feelings of friendship and patriotism." What it actually does is set theater back to prehistoric times by presenting such comical student-collaborated Hasty Pudding Theatricals as *The Jewel of Denial*, *It's a Wonderful Afterlife*, *Fangs For the Memories*, and *Snow Place Like Home*, set in a Catskills ski resort.

Infamous, as well, for its "Woman of the Year" award with annual presentations of the gold Hasty Pudding Pot to such notables as Katherine Hepburn, Angela Landsbury, and Carol Channing — escorted by college men in drag. And its annual "Man of the Year", roasts to honor distinguished gents dressed in wigs and custom bras, such as Kevin Kline in a "Wanda Bra", Mel Gibson in a "Cross Your Braveheart Bra", Billy Crystal in a "Miracle Maximizer Bra", and other gentlemen too chagrinned to mention.

Since Hasty Pudding tomfoolery didn't completely chafe the Harvard foundation, the little that remained was polished off in 1876 with the founding of the *Harvard Lampoon*, the self-proclaimed "world's oldest humor magazine," which dispenses irreverent wit and parody from its lofty mock-Flemish castle on campus. Today, the Lampoon society is notorious for its quarterly magazine, its annual parodies of other magazines such as *The Literary Digest*, *New Yorker*, *Playboy*, *USA Today*, and *Mademoiselle*, and its books *The Harvard Lampoon's Guide to College Admission* and *Bored of the Rings*, a Tolkien parody.

A Visit To the City

Going down to Boston from upcountry can be an engaging experience, particularly where the urban culture and the cost of that culture is the full-blown opposite of the rural way of life. Take Harry and Mary Babcock, who drove down for the annual flower show at the Massachusetts Horticultural Society. They enjoy the experience all right, but when they get back to Bill Peterson's Country Store to pick up their mail they're still a mite bedazzled by the experience.

"How was the traveling?" Bill inquires as they come in.

"When we got down there," Harry tells him, "We thought we were in a parking lot, but it turned out to be Kenmore Square."

"Did you look around the village any?" Bill asks.

"After seeing the flower show, we wandered about some," Harry replies, "but you know, by the time we were done, my five dollar bill was looking a mite peekid."

Get Scrod

The celebrated Parker House Hotel is renown for its Boston Cream Pie, Parker House dinner rolls and for Boston scrod, a term devised by the management to indicate "the fresh catch of the day." Since the dining room chefs had no idea ahead of time what fish species would be plentiful on a particular day, the management came up with this term to save on printing menus.

Years ago when the Boston & Maine Railroad used to bring folks down from upcountry to Boston's North Station, Edna Phelps in her younger days would make that trip faithfully each Saturday. Each time, Edna had noticed an elegant, elderly lady already onboard, but since they didn't know each other, they hadn't had an occasion to speak. Or so it was until this one time when the train was full, and Edna saw that the seat next to the lady had yet to be taken.

"I've seen you on this train over the years," Edna says to the lady.

"Yes," she replies, "and I've seen you, too."

"Do you enjoy the train?" Edna inquires.

"It's pleasant in its way," the lady replies. "I ride this train most every Saturday."

"Do you have relations in the city?" Edna asks.

"Oh, no," the lady replies, "I just go down to the Parker House to get scrod."

After a few moments of pondering, Edna finally comments, "I've been a school teacher for thirty-five years, and I never before knew what the past tense of that verb was."

The Holdup

Junior Coates is down Boston cutting across the Public Garden, when he is assaulted by two fellahs. Junior is a pretty rugged young man, so he puts up one wicked good fight. Finally though, the two fellahs finally subdue him and swipe the three dollars in his pocket.

"You sonuvabitch," one of the fellahs shouts at him, "You put up this battle over a miserable three bucks!"

"Gosh, I didn't know," Junior says, "I thought you wanted the twenty dollars in my shoe."

A Buck a Game

As you probably know, Walt Palmer is tight-fisted, consequently he's not much of a hand at staking anything other than a sure bet. He's been in Boston for a fisherman's conference at the Hotel Statler, and on his way back home, Walt, clad in his best flannel shirt and Sunday meeting trousers, sits next to a Bostonian dressed in a Brooks Brothers three-piece suit. Since there's some distance to travel, Walt and this Bostonian engage in some light conversation.

"You say you are a commercial fisherman," the Bostonian says after a spell, "I must tell you how impressed I am with both your wit and intelligence."

"That so?" says Walt.

"Yes, I am," the Bostonian says, "In fact, I'm so impressed that I'm going to make you a proposition."

"What proposition?" asks Walt, somewhat guarded.

"I propose we ask each other questions," the Bostonian says, "and the person who can't answer pays the other a dollar."

"Well, as you say, I'm a fisherman," Walt replies, "and since you are a sophisticated gentleman who is well-informed, having a wide range of experiences unknown to me, maybe we could even up the odds a mite."

"What do you have in mind?" the Bostonian asks.

"We'll keep the rules just as you suggest," says Walt, "except instead of me paying you a dollar, I'll just pay you fifty cents."

"That's fine with me," the Bostonian agrees, "I'll even allow you the first turn. Do you have a question in mind?"

"Well, here's one," says Walt, "What has three legs and flies?"

After the Bostonian had been silent a spell, chewing on the question, he finally admits he doesn't know and hands Walt a one-dollar bill.

"So?" the Bostonian asks, "What is it that has three legs and flies?"

"Darned if I know, mister," Walt says, "Here's your fifty cents."

The Prodigal Son

Joe Hancock works up to the Northwood Paper Company. Over the winter he's saved a sum that aches to be spent, so Joe decides to take a bus trip down to Boston.

On the morning of his journey, Matt Conley and Tom Lillibridge come by Bill Peterson's Country Store to see him off — and to offer advice like "Don't do anything I wouldn't do" and "Never use your real name."

Joe hasn't taken a bus before, so as he boards out front of the store, Frank Perry, the driver, asks him, "One way or round trip?"

"Round trip," Joe tells him.

"Where to?" Frank asks.

"Right back here," Joe replies.

This voyage isn't a religious pilgrimage, to be sure, and in a few hours time, Joe finds himself in that mecca of licentiousness, the Combat Zone, where iniquity's a commodity and spirits aren't holy.

After the week passes, Matt and Tom are sitting on the porch of Bill's store when the Trailways bus hauls up front, and Joe, spent and disoriented, stumbles onto the road.

"How'd it go?" Tom asks, "or don't you remember."

"Well, I'm flat broke," Joe says triumphantly. "I remember spending too much on liquor. I recall spending a wicked lot on women, but the rest of it — I'm not sure. The rest of it, I must have squandered."

Yankee Doodle

Yankee doodle came to town
  riding on a pony;
Stuck a feather in his hat,
  and called it macaroni.

First we'll take a pinch of snuff,
  and then a drink of water;
And then we'll say, "How do you do?"
  and that's a Yankee's supper.

Yankee doodle keep it up,
  Yankee doodle dandy;
Mind the music and the step,
  and with the girls be handy.

THESE MAY NOT SOUND LIKE FIGHTING WORDS, but if the New Englanders of this song weren't such dandies, they just might take their silk hankies and slap their accusers on the cheek. This ditty, despite its popularity with the playground set, is actually a political taunt by colonial revolutionaries against other colonists loyal to Great Britain.

In pre-revolutionary America the term *Yankee* was being used by British Redcoats against defiant New Englanders — the word having come from the Indian word *eankke*, meaning "coward". However, prior to the signing of the Declaration of Independence, the defiant colonists had adopted the moniker as a term meaning the antithesis of "British".

The Loyalists, however, weren't too convinced things were all that bad under the crown. After the infamous "Boston Tea Party" when tea taxed by Great Britain was illicitly chucked into Boston harbor by revolutionists led by brewer Samuel Adams (and disguised as Indians, an act of *eankke* to be sure) the Loyalists angrily pointed out that the price of tea was actually cheaper in Boston than in London. Nevertheless, those sewing the seeds of revolution taunted any colonist with a predisposition for things British.

"Doodle" is an old English verb meaning "to ridicule as foolish", even today doodling is to engage in trivial endeavors. Macaroni came to symbolize dandy cuisine and couture. And as you probably know, real men don't ride ponies.

13.
Naughty Stories

INITIALLY, MORAL EXPRESSION IN NEW ENGLAND was formed by Puritans, fundamentalist Protestants who treated sexuality as though it were something the Almighty created on a crazed day. In New England moral expression was further refined by the Shakers, other fundamentalist Protestants, who'd have chased the roosters from the hens, had it not screwed up egg production.

Then came the nineteenth century when New England's moral expression took an inspired turn with the arrival of those fun-loving Roman Catholic immigrants, the Irish, Italians, and Portuguese. Not to suggest these Catholics necessarily turned a blind eye to morality, they simply gave permission to Yankee Protestants to turn a blind eye.

Around this time in Boston, a temple was raised in Scollay Square by a reverent sect who'd sold their worldly wares, convinced the planet would meet its demise in April 1844. Apparently they were wrong, and now stuck on this mortal coil without a cent, they sell the place, and none too soon, either. The following year the structure's razed by fire, but soon after there's raised a new edifice made of fireproof Quincy granite, an irreverent tabernacle known as the Old Howard burlesque.

☛ Years ago "banned in Boston" was synonymous with old-time values and with the annihilation of all types of sophisticated entertainment in the city. That is, all but the Old Howard theater with its brassy burlesque shows featuring stunning chorus girls, famous strippers like Ann Corio and Irma the Body, stand-up comics like Lou Costello and Phil Silvers, and flirtatious sketches—

such as the buxomous beauty with bountiful bosoms, who faints onstage; whereupon a horde of gentlemen flock around her:

"What should we do?" a fellah cries out.

"Rub'er arms," shouts one.

"She won't come to," the fellah laments.

"Rub'er legs," suggests another.

"Oh, what can I do?" the fellah cries.

Just then a helium balloon vendor strolls by hollering, "Rubber balloons! Rubber balloons!"

The Old Howard was followed in the arena of adult entertainment by the notorious Combat Zone, the downtown district of erotic booksellers, sleazy strip clubs, and ladies selling their assets.

Henry Foster took a trip down there once, and then came home to talk about it. "I got me one of them downtown girls," he was saying, "and you know, if I'd've been just a mite bold, I would have kissed her."

The legacy of this turn in ethical events are naughty stories, which are okay to tell because they are traditional and in New England standing the test of time takes precedence over virtue.

A Whole New Crowd

Several of the fellahs are down Fred Johnson's Richfield filling station and garage sitting around shooting the breeze when talk gets going about whether there is more of it going on now than when all of us were young.

Some of them thought it was worse — what, you take some of those high school kids: they've got those hot rods, and they're out and around, a young fellah and a young girl. You can't be sure what they're doing, but whatever it is, you know it's not proper.

Then again there are other fellahs sitting around, and they think: don't know but what it's the same today.

Well, the debate goes back and forth like this, when after a spell Fred looks around and notices the oldest fellah there is Enoch Webster, who hasn't been saying too much.

"So, what you think, Enoch?" Fred asks him, "You think there's more of it now, than when we were all kids?"

"I don't know but that it's just about the same," he says, "but there's just one thing I don't like about it."

"What's that, Enoch?" asks Horace Peckham.

"Dammit," Enoch says, "There's a whole new crowd doing it."

What's It This Time, Junior

When Junior Coates got married and took his bride, Lulu, up Granite Mountain to the cabin he'd built, nobody was surprised when they stayed up there, occasionally coming down to Bill Peterson's Country Store for supplies. And it was usually an event, too, because each time they'd come down, there'd be another Coates added to the brood.

"So what's it this time?" someone would ask as they hauled up in front of the store.

"It's a boy," Junior would say, or "it's a girl", and so it went for a dozen years or more until that one trip down, when somebody asks the usual question.

"It ain't nothing," Junior replies. Well sir, if the folks standing about weren't all set a-back!

"What happened, Junior?" Tom Lillibridge asks, "There's nothing wrong, is there?"

"Oh, there ain't nothing wrong," Junior replies, "but you know something, after all these years we finally figured out what was causing that."

Go Fly a Kite

It's coming upon Snug Harbour Lobster Festival time again, and every year they have a kite fishing competition. Roger Hancock, when he was young, won it five years in a row. He's telling this to his boys, Joe and Kenny, over breakfast.

"You're a legend," Joe confirms.

"You think you still have it in you, Pa?" Kenny wants to know.

"Don't know but what I might," Roger brags.

So in short time, after Martha has a chance to clear the dishes, Roger, Joe, and Kenny are building a championship competition kite right there on the kitchen table. They get the main part completed and are just finishing up on the tail.

"It's too short, Roger," Martha says, "I think you need more tail."

"For heaven's sake, Martha, make up your mind," he replies, "Last night you told me to go fly a kite."

Nice Day For It

Downeast on the Maine coast is a small skiff called a punt, the name derived from the old French word for a flat-bottom boat with a squared-off fore and aft. The punt of this story is the small rowing skiff that's become common on the New England coast.

It's with slight apprehension Walt Palmer is sculling about Salt Cove tonging quahaugs when he notices a punt adrift. Small punts, as you may know, are rarely used by working fishermen because they aren't hardy enough for the rigors of lobstering or shellfishing, but they are sometimes used by divers as they clean boat bottoms of barnacles and other sea growth.

As Walt continues tonging in the warmth of the morning sun, he slowly works his way toward the little punt, figuring it to be the manual arts project of some Northwood Academy boy, who hadn't considered the rising tide when stowing her on the beach.

After a spell, Walt hauls up along side and sees he's partially right, because there on the bottom of that little punt is Jeremiah Coates and some high school girl going at it — not that it fazes Walt any. He just looks down at them and says, "You sure got a nice day for it."

The Surprise Party

Spud and Isabelle Carpenter are having their fiftieth wedding anniversary, so the folks up to the Congregational Meeting House thought it would be nice to throw them a surprise party, but no one was too sure how to go about it without letting one or the other in on it. It's the Reverend Powell who suggests Isabelle ought to know, so they get to talking to her, and get the plans figured out. Everyone will bring a covered dish, a pie, or some such to eat.

They have decided the best time to assemble at the farmhouse is while Spud's out to the barn doing evening chores, so they all wait just over the brow of the hill where they can see him, but he can't see them. Soon as Spud's inside the barn, they flock like mosquitoes onto that farmhouse. They get themselves hidden behind the walnut sofa, the plush chairs, and the other furniture in the parlor for when Spud comes back inside.

The first thing he does when he comes in is to go into the parlor and light that kerosene oil heater of his. The folks are hidden around as Spud takes the Mason jar of wooden matches, strikes one on the zipper of his pants, but the spark goes out. As a matter of fact, Spud breaks two or three of those wooden matches before he finally looks up toward the kitchen where Isabelle is pretending to fix supper.

"You know something, Isabelle," Spud hollers, "There ain't near so much fire in my pants as there were fifty years ago tonight."

Got the Grippe

It's been three or four months since Joe Hancock took his decadent little vacation down Boston. Well, one evening all of a sudden a long distance telephone call comes in for him.

"Undertaker", Joe answers, "You plug 'em; we plant 'em."

"This you, Joey?" a female voice drifts from the other end of the line.

"Yes, 'tis," Joe replies.

"This is Rosie down in Boston," she says.

"Gosh," says Joe, "I don't know any Rosie down in Boston."

"For heaven's sake, Joey," she replies, "Don't you remember that night we met on Boston Common? We got to talking, then we ended up in your room at the Earle Hotel, and we had us a *real* lofty time?"

"I certainly do remember, Rosie," Joe says, "and how have you been?"

"Well, that's what I'm calling about, Joey, I'm kinda worried," she tells him, "To tell you the truth that was almost four months ago, and I haven't been sick since then."

"Gosh Rosie, aren't you lucky," Joe replies, "Why, everybody up here's got the grippe."

In the Hay Loft

Do you remember that time when *The Northwood Independent* sent their reporter around to interview Edna Phelps on the occasion of her ninety-first birthday? Well, while they were talking, Edna got a mite confused.

"You ever been sick, Miss Phelps?" the reporter asks her.

"No," Edna tells him, "I've never been sick."

"And you've never been to the hospital?" the reporter inquires.

"No," she replies, "I've never been to the hospital."

"So, you've never been bedridden?" the reporter asks.

"No, I haven't," Edna replies, "Though I did get it twice in the hay loft."

128   *New England Tall Tales & White Lies*

An advertising card from the long-ago New England Fair. Today the Skowhegan Fair in Maine, Topsfield Fair in Massachusetts, and Brooklyn Fair in Connecticut all claim to be "America's Oldest Fair."

14.
The County Fair

AT THE ADVENT OF THE TWENTIETH CENTURY there were throughout the countryside evangelists preaching that giants dwell at the center of the earth. They'd taken this notion from Genesis 6 that speaks of a giant race called the Nephilim, and this gives archeologist George Hull an idea.

He buys a twelve-foot slab of gypsum with dark veins and hires a master stonecutter to carve a giant man with all the necessary bits like toenails, nostrils, sex organs, and a right hand clutching his stomach. The giant man is "aged" with ink and sulfuric acid and is buried near an authentic fossil site near Cardiff in upstate New York.

After the petrified man was "discovered", the Cardiff Giant, as the newspapers christened him, is put on display at twenty-five cents admission — soon raised to fifty cents by the notoriety. Mr. Hull quickly becomes a wealthy man.

Over the line in New England and unbeknown to Mr. Hull a politician named Phineas Taylor Barnum had copied the giant man and was soon displaying the Cardiff Giant, claiming his was the original and the other one was fake. He was sued, naturally, but the judge threw out the case convinced both were hoaxes.

P. T. Barnum soon after becomes mayor of Bridgeport, Connecticut then creates the American Museum of oddities — many fake — and finally teams up with circus impresario James Bailey to form "Barnum & Bailey's Greatest Show On Earth." After his death in 1891, Barnum's Cardiff Giant was displayed for many years at Connecticut's late Great Danbury Fair.

☞ The Great Danbury Fair in Danbury, Connecticut was arguably New England's finest, having begun in 1821 as a typical community event and soon growing into a major attraction for both locals and city families from nearby New York. Even schools and factories took time off come fairtime.

In 1946 John Leahey, a local fuel oil dealer, purchased the fairgrounds and threw his heart and capital into it. Over the years the fair evolved beyond typical agricultural competitions and exhibitor booths into an entertainment funland of Mr. Leahey's creation and included a daily grand parade led by Mr. Leahey in his radiant ringmaster's uniform.

After Mr. Leahey died in 1974, the fair limped along without direction until 1981 when it finally succumbed to neglect and plundering by the management. The fairground was sold, leveled and was soon reinvented as the Danbury Fair shopping mall.

Democrat Pies

Having begun in 1878 on the village green in Rumford Falls, the annual County Agricultural Fair holds forth at the end of each September, and has since spread down the hill behind the Town House and into the hayfields beyond. Each year there are various farm animal shows, cooking competitions, quilting contests, and special attractions including a Fair Queen beauty pageant, though beauty hardly ever enters into it. Just at the edge of the fairgrounds, where the hill begins its downward grade, the Republican Ladies League operates a fresh-baked pie stand.

After helping his brother with his family's cattle in the show arena, Joe Hancock approaches the pie booth, his mind set on a slice of their hot, deep-dish apple pie with homemade vanilla ice cream onto it.

"I'm sorry, Joe," apologizes Mary Babcock, who's serving patrons at the counter, "I'm afraid our apple pies are only half-baked."

"Half-baked?" Joe repeats, smiling.

"They'll be ready in about twenty minutes," Mary assures him.

"If they're only half-baked," Joe replies, "Don't know but what you got there are some of them Democrat pies."

The Barnstormer

With the advent of aviation during World War I when the Army Air Corp trained scores of pilots, there were countless aviators around with the passion for flying, the bravery for the task, and after the war no place to perform. Since there were many folks back home who'd read news accounts about these heroic young warriors of the skies and were curious to witness their derring-do, entertainment ventures were launched as these young pilots brought flying stunt shows to fairs and aerodromes around the country.

One such "barnstormer", as they were called, came up to the County Agricultural Fair in Rumford Falls last autumn, and since the folks over Center Northwood were carrying on so much about it, Henry Foster and Enoch Webster figured they best go see what all the fuss was about.

Most of the fairgoers had already packed into the grandstand by the time Henry and Enoch get there, but since the aeroplane was just setting on the dirt racetrack in front of the stands, they manage to squeeze in at the fence to get a good view.

At two o'clock prompt, the pilot, dressed in a shiny leather flying costume with a striking red scarf, saunters out before a cheering crowd, fiddles with a few things, and hops into the cockpit. Then another fellah comes out in dazzling white coveralls and gets the propeller spinning. VA-AH-AH-ROOOM! The engine roars to life as a hush of anticipation settles over the crowd. By now everyone to a man is on his feet, as the flying machine starts to move along the racetrack.

"Hard to fathom he gets that off the ground," Henry says.

"He hasn't yet," Enoch reminds him.

Just then, that aeroplane sets aloft to the thundering ovation of the grandstand crowd. At first he just circles the fairgrounds, making passes over the center oval, barely missing the cars parked on the infield. Then the pilot does some gigantic loop-the-loops, follows with terrifying barrel rolls, then as a grand finale, the young pilot engages in what the program calls "The Falling Leaf" — the crowd shrieking with pleasure then gasping in fright.

"How'd you like to be up there with him?" Henry asks Enoch.

"I'd rather be up there with him than without him," he replies.

Pig To the Fair

Spud Carpenter wants to enter one of his pigs in the swine competition up to the County Agricultural Fair, but as the time closes in, he's taken ill with the collywobbles, so Junior Coates offers to take the pig over for him.

By noontime the ailment broke, so Spud and Isabelle decide to drive over to the fairground to see how Junior's getting on. As they take the bend over by the Congregational Meeting House, they see Junior leading that pig right down through Center Northwood.

"I thought you were taking my pig over the fairgrounds," Spud inquires from the driver's window.

"I did, Mr. Carpenter, and we had a swell time," Junior tells him, "Now we're headed over Bill Peterson's store for penny candy."

Matt's Racing Cow

Right before Matt Conley married Mary Ann, he bought Fairview Farm from Seth Thayer's son, Nate — this was right after Seth had fallen off the barn roof and busted his neck. Matt's a lobsterman, you know, so he didn't know much about farming and struggled with it some.

After a spell, Matt thought he should buy himself a cow for no better reason than most the farms around here have cows. Since he didn't have much money after buying the place, Matt went up to see Josiah Coates, figuring he would set him the best deal. So Matt dickers some on the price and finally comes away with a lean little heifer — though she looks more like a deer than any cow. Right off he names her Mary Ann, after that girl who's been chasing him.

Matt gets the cow down to his farm, but that first time he opens the barn door, she breaks right out from the stanchion and shoots down the Coast Road, hell bent and on a run. He had to walk down three miles or some to catch her and bring her back to the barn.

Well, Matt beefs up that old barn door of his, but the next morning, the same thing, and this gives Matt an idea. He gets down that old racing sulky of Seth's and the next morning he gets out there before Mary Ann has a chance to break out of the barn. He hooks her up to that sulky and off they go. After a spell, Matt gets Mary Ann trained so he can guide her some, and every morning they'd get out there on the Coast Road and go four or five miles and back again.

It finally comes around for the County Agricultural Fair, and Matt sees in *The Northwood Independent* they have a final class called a free-for-all race open to any racing animal, and it has a purse of one hundred dollars. Well, Matt gets up to the fairgrounds early, and he tethers Mary Ann to a pine tree back there. Then he gets the sulky hitched up, so as that bell sounds off, Matt casts off the tether and aims for the track.

Well, Mary Ann breaks right through that fence and gets going all stretched out on that track. The crowd's all watching the horses clearing the first turn until they see this cow come through the starting gate, her horns lowered, and that milk bag swinging from side to side. You should have heard them holler!

Mary Ann overhauls that last horse something wicked, and when she come along side, that horse smells something peculiar and breaks gait, heading right out through the fence. And that's how it went all along that second turn. Every time Mary Ann overhauls one of those horses, it shears off and breaks right through the fence. By the time she overhauls that last horse just before the finish line, he shears off, but that cow won't stop.

After she clears the finish line, Mary Ann heads around that track a second time, so by the time she comes back to the finish line there's a flock of folks crowded onto the track.

"Look out for that cow!" somebody hollers.

Just then someone throws a horse blanket over her head, but that just blinds her, naturally. Mary Ann shears through the backside, and runs through the infield and into a flivver parked there. Matt, he falls out and lands on the ground half-dead, but that cow, she just disappears on a run.

"There's nothing wrong with that money you made for me today," Matt says as he starts to come to.

Just then that girl Mary Ann runs up. "Matt, Matt, you all right?" she's yelling.

"Mary Ann, my darling, you did mighty good today," Matt says, "I'll grain and pasture you all your days."

"I knew you were contemplating matrimony," she says, "and today, too!"

So, Matt Conley gets himself betrothed before he has a mind too.

The Purple Balloon

Spud and Isabelle Carpenter's grandson, Johnny, spent the night Saturday at their farm. His folks had dropped him off after being up the fairground all afternoon, and for a while before bedtime he was playing with a purple balloon his father had bought him up to the fair.

Since it'd been warm all day, Isabelle had left the windows and doors open, so during the night that balloon kinda drifts around in the breeze, one room to the next, and finally into his grandparent's bedroom, landing in their armchair commode.

During the night Isabelle had occasion to use the commode, but it isn't until morning that she notices it's all purple. Naturally, that unhinges her a mite, so she calls Dr. Kenny, who really doesn't recognize this from any of his experience. Eventually, he determines the only reasonable thing to do is to come by and have a look.

After Dr. Kenny arrives and has observed as much as can be seen, he takes a probe from his black bag and begins poking at it. BANG!

"Godfrey!" hollers Isabelle, taken aback. "What the devil's that?"

"Well, I can't be sure," Dr. Kenny tells her, "but between you and me, I believe we are the only two to ever see a fart."

The Aeroplane Ride

A bunch of us are up to Bill Peterson's Country Store. The fellahs are gathered in the warmth of his old potbelly woodstove talking about nothing in particular when we fetch upon the subject of money and who might be the tightest fellah in town.

"Walt Palmer, no doubt," Tom Lillibridge says.

"No, sir," some of the other fellahs say, then they start giving testimonies of penny-pinching, each claiming to be more tight-fisted than the next. Finally, it comes around to Matt Conley.

"Remember that aviator fellah up the fair last summer?" Matt says, "After each performance he'd come down onto that back stretch of racetrack in the outfield.

"Well, my wife and I, we just happened to come along, so we go over, and you know what? That pilot offers to take us up in his aeroplane, if I'd pay him ten dollars.

"'That's too steep for me,' I said to him, but since he didn't have anything else to do until the next performance, he said he'd take us up, and so long as we didn't scream or yell or anything, he wouldn't charge for the ride.

"Well, no sooner as he gets us up he commences to dive right for the top of Granite Mountain, then he quick pulls up and makes a bunch of spins and rolls, then he turns upside down and flies under that trestle down Wood River, finally leveling off over Arrow Lake and bringing her around and back onto that stretch of racetrack at the fairground again.

"After I hop out, the pilot asks me if I was ever scared or felt like hollering or something. 'No,' I tell him, 'except maybe that time you flew upside-down under the trestle, and Mary Ann fell out.'"

Post Time

It's right before post time down to the fairground racetrack and Junior Coates is standing at the cage, racing form in hand, putting all his money on the sorriest horse of the pack.

"Why are you betting on that broken down nag?" Horace Peckham asks, "It'll probably be hauled off for mucilage by the end of this race."

"The form here says it's starting out at twenty to one," Junior tells him, "The rest of them don't get started 'til fifteen past one."

Right or Left?

Matt Conley's been to sea long enough to know that once a boat's named, it's bad luck to change it; but a cow, well that's an udderly different matter. So what with his new bride, Mary Ann, resenting having his prize-winning racing cow named after her, Matt renames the cow Daisy — not that he has a mind one way or t'other.

"Yessah, Mary Ann's got herself in a real snit over it," Matt says. He's out with Joe Hancock in his pickup truck with Daisy running along behind. "She didn't mind I named the boat after her, though."

"Then tell her you named the cow after the boat," Joe replies. They'd been driving along twenty miles an hour when Joe speeds to twenty-five. "She's keeping up," he reports.

"Then goose 'er some more," Matt suggests.

"You sure?" Joe asks, looking through the rear view mirror, "Her tongue's already sticking out of her mouth."

"Right or left?" Matt asks.

"Left," Joe tells him.

"Pull over," Matt says, "She wants to pass."

Snug Harbour and Whaler's Inn.

15.
Gone Huntin'

SPORTS FISHERMEN OFTEN BOAST of the leviathan that got away, but one of the tallest of New England fish tales — and there are those who'd swear on *Ripley's Believe It Or Not!* it's true — is the venerable monster of Lake Champlain.

There's hardly a man nor boy who is not familiar with the monster of Loch Ness in Scotland — known as "Nessie", recognized widely by raw photographs, and yet elusive despite numerous attempts to document its existence. Well sir, the creature's lineage apparently extends beyond those shores to northern New England.

Lake Champlain is one hundred, twenty-five miles long, forming a tenable moat between New England and upstate New York. Although it has never been designated a Great Lake, Lake Champlain interconnects with those other five and is the sixth largest fresh-water body in the United States. Loch Ness by comparison is merely twenty-four miles long, yet both drops to a depth of about four hundred, thirty feet and are slightly acidic, having both been inlets of the North Atlantic Ocean.

The Champlain monster, known popularly as "Champ", was first sighted by native Abenaki and Iroquois, were chronicled by French explorer Samuel de Champlain in 1609, and has since been sighted no less than three-hundred times. Both the Vermont and New York state legislatures have, in fact, enacted legislation protecting Champ.

Knowing this, keep in mind that moose are great swimmers and are often spotted swimming across the lake. Also keep in mind that moose don't always have antlers. And keep in mind that many of the pleasure craft motoring on Lake Champlain are floating cocktail lounges, which possibly explains away many of these sightings.

☞ As the first autumn snow settles upon placid woodlands, frozen ponds, and those rural upcountry roads with BRAKE FOR MOOSE signs, many of the seasonal businesses around the Western Lakes Region of Maine and elsewhere throughout New England shut down so hunting can commence.

"See those?" Roger Hancock asks his younger son, Kenny, as they track game in the snow, "Your supper's at the other end."

Soon after, as village folks decorate their porches with ears of Indian corn, jack-o-lanterns, and bundled cornstalks, upcountry folks festoon their porches with hanging deer carcasses — venison curing in the autumn cold, shielded from the bore of predators.

Hunting in these dank north woods, particularly during an afternoon thaw, prompts dampness to set into leather boots causing woolen socks to absorb like wicks. This isn't merely wet and uncomfortable, but it also raises frostbite. So whereas necessity is the mother of invention, its father in this case is a man called Leon Leonwood Bean, who in 1911 invented a boot that combines breathable leather tops with waterproof rubber bottoms. He called his boots The Maine Hunting Shoe™, and opened a shop on Main Street in Freeport.

By 1964 Mr. Bean's store had greatly expanded, attracting sportsmen twenty-four hours a day, three-hundred, sixty-five days a year, stocking up on supplies, purchasing equipment, and obtaining hunting and fishing licenses. Or it did until somebody noticed a Blue Law requiring stores to be closed on Sundays. That took a couple weeks of prayer and politics to sort out.

Today, L. L. Bean is just down Main Street occupying a nearly one hundred, twenty thousand square foot store with an indoor trout pond, plus the company has several branch stores, an immense mail order business, and internet customers worldwide.

Henry's Hunting Trip

Last Saturday was a fine day, what with blue skies, crisp air, and just a hint of a breeze, so Henry Foster figures if he's going to lay in game for the winter, this would be a good time to head out. After fetching his shotgun, the one with the double barrels, he hops into his truck and drives to the woodlands up past Arrow Lake.

Luck isn't with him, though, so after sitting up a tree by a deer run most of the afternoon and not seeing a damn thing, Henry decides at around dusk to track around by Wood River on his way back to his truck. He's down to Bill Peterson's Country Store telling some of the fellahs about this afterwards.

"So you got anything to show for this besides a sore tail from settin' up that tree?" Bill wants to know.

"As I came around the hill there," Henry says, "I spot a twelve point buck just at the edge of the clearing, so I take careful aim and am close to pulling the trigger when I see from the corner of my eye a bull moose stepping out from a stand of pines. I aim precisely between them and squeeze both triggers in quick succession. BOOM, BOOM!

"The bullets ricochet off a granite ledge, killing both the buck and the moose. The recoil kicks me back into the river, and when I came to, my right hand is clutching a rabbit's tail, my left hand is grasping a mallard's neck, and the pockets of my britches are so full of trout that the buttons pop off my fly and kill two pheasants."

The Breakfast Sausages

One of the rites of passage upcountry is scaling fish, plucking fowl, and skinning deer, which Roger Hancock had learned well in his younger days. As a matter of fact, most the meat he's ever eaten is game he or his boys had shot and cleaned themselves. So it's with uncertain bewilderment that Roger and his sons sit down to breakfast after coming in from chores one morning.

"What you suppose it is?" asks Joe, his oldest, gazing at their plates.

"Golly, I don't know," Roger replies, "Ma, what're these little turds on our plates?"

"Now Roger, those are sausages," Martha replies, "I bought them down to Bill Peterson's store."

"What's a sausage, Pa?" Kenny, his younger boy, wants to know.

"Can't say as I'm sure," Roger says.

"Smells good," Joe says as he picks one up with his fork and bites into it, "It tastes pretty good, too."

"There's just one thing, though," Roger comments, "After she cleaned them, there's not much left."

Brake For Moose

There's getting to be quite a heap of moose around here, so many that the government's considering extending the hunting season just to thin out the stock. Moose, if you don't already know, don't see too good, particularly at night. When there are headlights coming at them, instead of freezing in the road like deer do, moose will charge. Nobody has to tell you what damage a couple thousand pounds of moose can do to the front end of a car.

One evening last week a Massachusetts fellah was ripping up North Road when he comes upon a bull moose at the curve right by Josiah Coates's old trailer. Being from away, the fellah doesn't know to brake and shut off the headlights, so that old moose charges him down and ends up wrapped all over that fellah's car.

Hearing the ruckus, Josiah comes out on a trot to the road.

"You thumped a moose," Josiah says. The fellah's mighty distraught, as you can imagine.

"I didn't see him," the fellah cries.
"He saw you," Josiah says.
"You think I hurt him?" the fellah wants to know.
"I don't suppose you done him no good," Josiah replies.

The Potluck Beans

Patience Powell, the minister's wife, is famous for her homemade baked beans, and every church potluck supper, she's expected to bring a pot of those beans. As a matter of fact there's a supper Friday night, and she's already got a pot of beans soaking on the kitchen table.

The partridge season's just starting and her husband, the Reverend Preston Powell, has been invited to join Roger Hancock and a couple of church members, so he's sitting at the opposite end of the kitchen table getting ready when a wicked sneeze gets him. Godfrey mighty, birdshot scatters all over that kitchen, a few landing in the beans soaking on the table. Because he's so intent on cleaning shot off the floor, Reverend Powell doesn't notice any went into the beans, or at least he doesn't until the day following the potluck supper.

"Those beans last night," he says to Patience, "What did you put in them?"

"The same as usual," she tells him, "Why do you ask?"

"This morning when I bent over to pick up the newspaper," he says, "I passed wind and blew a hole in my good trousers."

Hunting Bear

Tom Lillibridge, Joe Hancock, and Matt Conley are planning their annual hunting trip, when Matt has the inspiration to invite along his young hire hand, Tony Briggs, who for the whole of his life has hardly been out of town, much less hunting.

They rent a cabin in the north country, get licenses, and pay the Northwood Paper Company the fee to use their logging roads, then they're off in Matt's pick-up truck loaded with gear, periodically switching off since only two fellahs can fit into the cab at a time.

The morning after they arrive to the cabin, Tony, filled with the fellah's stories of previous hunting trips and embolden from their drinking whiskey late into the night before, enthusiastically sets out before the others have even come awake.

In mighty short time Tony fixes upon a tremendous bear strolling toward the lake, so he quickly raises his gun and in so doing attracts the attention of the bear, which takes chase. With all his youthful might, Tony springs for that cabin, the bear close on his heels.

Just as he gets the cabin door open, Tony trips on the threshold, which causes him to stumble and for the bear to trip over him. That tremendous bear did a flip, landing square in the center of the cabin floor. Tony quickly springs to his feet, slams the door shut from the outside, then shouts through the open window, "Here's your bear, fellahs. You skin him, while I fetch another."

Shot For Grouse

There's a substantial industry upcountry, apart from summer tourists, autumn foliage gazers, and winter sports enthusiasts that caters to the wants and demand of visiting sportsmen. Bait shacks, equipment rentals, guide services, hunting camps, and any number of supply merchants.

So it is that an out-of-towner called to the north woods for bird hunting hauls up to the counter of Bill Peterson's Country Store seeking ammunition.

"Do you have any shot for grouse?" the out-of-towner inquires.

"What you looking for?" Bill asks.

"Shot for grouse," the out-of-towner repeats, "Do you have any shot for grouse?"

"Gawd, fellah," Bill replies, "Don't you mean cartridges for partridges?"

The Big Catch

Some time ago Josiah Coates figured his life was just too rough a row to hoe and decides to end it. He rides down Bill Peterson's Country Store on that bicycle of his, buys himself a small tin of turpentine, a jug of kerosene, a box of matches, and a long length of rope, then he peddles down to Wood River.

When he gets to the cliff by the Boston & Maine Railroad trestle, Josiah ties one end of the rope around his neck, throws the other end over the trestle, and ties that to a white birch tree on the river bank. Then Josiah drinks down most of the turpentine, pours the kerosene over his clothes, lights it, and jumps off the cliff out over the river.

Horace Peckham is doing some fly-fishing on the other side when he takes notice of Josiah, and relays this tale later over coffee down Lew Cottrell's Minuteman Diner.

Well sir, Josiah's noose is tied so poorly it slips off his neck immediately sending him plunging into the river. The plunge puts out the flames, and sinks him almost to the bottom.

On his way back up he sucks in so much water that when he surfaces, Josiah commences to coughing and hacking so badly he heaves up all the turpentine causing a phosphorescent slick on the surface of the river. Then he drifts into Horace's line.

By the time Horace manages to cross the trestle, nearly getting knocked off by a freight train heading upcountry, he is nearly out of breath himself and not particularly sure what to do. There stands Josiah, naked as the day he was born, tangled in fishing line, and looking a mite dazed.

"You all right?" Horace asks him.

"You know, if I warn't such a good swimmer," Josiah brags, "I think I just might've drowned."

The Tremendous Ol' Bear

Tom Lillibridge, Joe Hancock, Matt Conley, and Tony Briggs are just back from their hunting trip up north. They settle in by the warm potbelly woodstove in Bill Peterson's Country Store and begin unwinding their tale of why they've come back scratched up and empty-handed.

According to their version of events, they'd been out tracking bear when they fix upon filling their water bottles. Closing in on the lake, they suddenly come upon a tremendous ol' bear squatting there in the water.

"Don't worry," Tom shouts to the other fellahs, "He's as afraid of you as you are of him."

"If that's true," replies Matt, "then that water's not fit to drink."

Just then, that tremendous ol' bear leaps onto his feet and lunges for them.

"Now what're we gonna do?" cries Tony.

"I'll show you what were gonna do," yells Tom, and with those words he thrusts his hand right down that bear's throat, through his intestines, and right out t'other end. With considerable determination, Tom grabs that ol' bear's tail, gives it one mighty yank, pulling that bear completely inside out.

"Golly," says Josh Peckham, Horace's boy, who is hanging on every word. By now other folks have gathered around.

"That bear realizes he'd met his match," Tom tells the folks, "so he decides the only thing for him to do is to make one fast retreat, which he does, running back-asswards into the woods."

16.
The Farm

SINCE MEDIEVAL TIMES farmers have relied on almanacs to calculate the germination and growth of crops, and so among New England's oldest and most informative publications is the *Farmers Almanac* — both of them.

The *Old Farmers Almanac* was started by Robert B. Thomas in 1792 with the stated purpose "to be useful, but with a pleasant degree of humour." The *Farmers Almanac* was founded by David Young and Jacob Mann in 1818 with the continued purpose to "forever capture the hearts and minds of young and old."

The word "almanac" derives from the Arabic word for weather, and weather predictions continue to drive both of New England's venerable publications. Using guidelines based on astronomical calculations, skilled guesswork, and chance — by "Abe Weatherwise" and "Caleb Weatherbee", respectively — both almanacs incorporate monthly forecasts along with astronomical charts, planting cycles, household tips, prominent dates, historical trivia, and wit.

The *Old Farmers Almanac* continues publishing annually in Dublin, New Hampshire. The *Farmers Almanac* likewise publishes each year in Lewiston, Maine.

☛ In the early days of the twentieth century popular music was distributed not on phonograph records, cassette tapes, or compact discs, but as sheet music to be played on a piano at home or at community gatherings such as the Elks, Odd Fellows, and the Grange. The songs were primarily ballads, often tear-jerkers, with long stories and equally long titles, such as *Come After Breakfast, Bring Your Own Lunch, and Leave Before Suppertime*. Or that memorable Prohibition tune, *Oh You Don't Need Wine To Have a Wonderful Time (While They Still Make Those Beautiful Girls)*.

It's fortunate these songs were distributed as sheet music since the titles wouldn't have fit on records, tapes, or CDs. One soulful song from the era is a ballad about a farm girl who gets a taste of big city life:

> *Aren't you coming back to old New Hampshire, Molly?*
> *Aren't you coming back to see us on the farm?*
> *The folks all say, "You won't be back,"*
>   *"You won't be back,"*
>   *"You won't be back."*
> *But something seems to tell me that you love me,*
>   *As you did before you went away to roam.*
> *So, aren't you coming back to old New Hampshire, Molly?*
> *Aren't you coming back to see us on the farm?*

This type of song was typical as American society was quickly turning from agrarian to industrial and as the children of the farm soon sought the perceived benefits of the city. Some of these children soon strayed, however, working the cold New York streets, particularly Broadway, a street that *Daily Mirror* columnist Walter Winchell called "the hardened artery":

> *Mabel Brown went to town,*
>   *all dressed up in her gingham gown;*
> *With a ribbon in her hair,*
>   *in her eyes a vacant stare.*
> *She joined a show, wrote her beau,*
>   *Mabel wanted to let him know;*
> *She is earning (so to speak)*
>   *twenty dollars a week.*

Her beau came down to New York town
  to see his Mabel dear;
The moment that he saw her flat,
  he whispered in her ear:
"How do you do it, Mabel,
  on twenty dollars a week?
"Tell me how you are able,
  on twenty dollars a week.
"A fancy flat and a diamond bar,
  twenty hats and a motor car!
"Go right to it, but how do you do it,
  on twenty dollars a week?"

I Had A Car Like That

This last time Enoch Webster was down Texas, his old Army buddy drove him around his vast cattle ranch. As they're driving, his buddy inquired about Enoch's dairy farm up New England.

"My farm's been in our family seven generations," Enoch tells him, "and I suppose it's something like six hundred acres, if you count the frog pond."

"Why that's a mighty small spread," his buddy comments, "Why, my ranch is so large, it takes me all day to drive around it."

"I know what you mean," Enoch replies, "I had a car like that once, but I sold it."

Bull Powder

Josiah Coates is having trouble with those cows he keeps up there on Granite Mountain. Seems milk production is off, so he gets Enoch Webster, a real dairyman, to come check them out.

"There's nothing wrong with your cows," Enoch tells him, "It's your bull — his sexual drive's off."

"What can I do about it?" Josiah wants to know.

"Fetch a bucket of water," Enoch tells him.

After Josiah gets back with the bucket, Enoch pours in some powder from a canning jar he'd brought with him and mixes it up in the water.

"Now we've got to get that bull to drink this down," Enoch says.

Well, the bull sniffs at the mixture then swigs it down with no encouragement at all. In next to no time his head rears up, and he breaks away, jumps the stonewall, and services all those cows that very afternoon.

Josiah is telling this down to Bill Peterson's Country Store.

"So what's in that powder?" Bill wants to know.

"I don't know," says Josiah, "but it tastes licorice."

Matt's Dry Well

Matt Conley is suffering kind of a dry spell at his house. You remember that Matt bought Fairview Farm after Seth Thayer's accident.

"Seth mostly lived there all by himself," Matt was telling Tom Lillibridge, "and when I first moved in, I was mostly living alone, too."

"Then you married Mary Ann," Tom says.

"We began having friends over, you know," Matt says, "Seems there's always folks around — and that's when my well water started tasting foul."

"What'd you do about it?" Tom asks.

"I bottled up a sample of the water," Matt says, "and sent it off to that laboratory down Boston along with a detailed letter."

"Hear back yet?" Tom inquires.

"They said the well's too close to my leach field," Matt says, "So I dug a cesspool further down behind the house."

"That solved it, right?" Tom asks.

"Nope," Matt says, "When I switched over to the cesspool, the well dried up."

Three Dollars Enough?

Edna Phelps lives out the Coast Road, and she's always been sort of an independent type. But now that she's ninety-one, she's having to modify her lifestyle somewhat, and one thing she's trying to work out is what to do with her garbage without having to cart the stuff up to the town dump in her car. She was discussing her predicament with Bill Peterson at his country store on her last trip up the Center.

"You know what you can do, Edna," Bill suggests partly in jest, "You can get yourself a pig to eat up all that garbage."

Not knowing a thing about it, she takes his advice seriously and calls Roger Hancock, who sells her a young sow for five dollars. Well, it arrives a little piggy, but it eventually turns from squiggly pink to shaggy gray and routs out nearly every blade of grass between the picket fence and the house. Finally, Edna figures what with winter coming, she best call Roger, which she does, telling him how well her pig has done but now come and take it away.

Next morning Roger shows up with his sons Joe and Kenny along with Tom Lillibridge to load this critter onto the truck. Pigs are a lot smarter than most people think, and it's no easy matter loading a hog onto a farm truck for that one last ride.

After they get the job done, Roger hands some cash to Joe and sends him up to settle with Edna, who still doesn't grasp the concept. As Joe hauls up to Edna's house, she hauls out onto the porch.

"Since I had the use of it all summer," she says to Joe, "Do you suppose three dollars is too much to ask?"

There's More To Life

Enoch Webster is a dairy farmer, you know, and he's putting in a new field of alfalfa by the road leading to his barn. Soon, Walt Palmer comes along and spots Enoch plowing the field with his bull.

"What the hell are you doing?" Walt inquires.

"You can see what I'm doing," Enoch replies.

"I mean, you've got a tractor," Walt says, "So why are you plowing with your bull?"

"You know something, Walt," Enoch tells him, "It's important this bull understands there's more to life than just romance."

Stonewalls

As a small indication of the far-reaching popularity of New England humor stories, an Atlanta newscaster told a version of this yarn on **WSB-TV**. Even deep in Rebel country — home to the resolute General Thomas "Stonewall" Jackson — the symbol that best characterizes New England is its ubiquitous stonewalls.

Spud Carpenter is out plowing his potato field when a tourist car pulls up, and the driver shouts something from his car window. Spud can't hear him, so he continues plowing figuring if it's important, the damn fool will get out of his car and walk over. Which he does.

"I have a question," the tourist shouts to him.

"Go ahead," Spud yells back.

"Why do New England farmers use stonewalls?" the tourist wants to know.

Since Spud was born and raised on this very farm, he'd never given it any thought. Around these parts folks mostly use what's at hand, and one thing that's at hand is plenty of rocks. So that's what Spud tells him.

"Then, where did all the rocks come from?" the tourist wants to know.

Spud hadn't given that much thought, either. He did recall from his days at Arrow Lake Grammar School being told about a great glacier that plowed south from the North Pole pushing rocks down to what is now New England. So that's what he tells the tourist.

"Well, then," the tourist continues, "Where's the glacier now?"

By now Spud's had enough of the questions and just wants get back to plowing.

"So far as I know," Spud replies, "it's up north now fetching more rocks."

Stud Service

Right after he gets that bull functioning again, Josiah Coates decides to hire it out for stud. Ten dollars a day is what he's charging, and he's even put up a notice on the bulletin board down Bill Peterson's Country Store.

One afternoon a fellah makes his way up North Road to where Josiah has nailed a sign to a tree that says "Stud Service" with an arrow pointing down the path to his trailer. The fellah gets out of his truck and bangs on Josiah's door.

"Go away!" Josiah hollers from inside.

"I need to talk to you," the fellah yells back.

Josiah opens the door and peeks out.

"Your son, Jeremiah," the fellah says, "He's been having relations with my daughter."

"Gawd, I don't know," says Josiah.

"Well, what are you going to do about it?" the fellah demands.

"I charge ten dollars for the bull," Josiah says, "I don't know what to get for Jeremiah."

The Time of Day

Enoch Webster's out in the field milking a cow one afternoon when a driver in a Cadillac pulls to the side of the road by the pasture gate. "You wouldn't happen to know what time it is, would you?" the driver inquires.

After feeling around the udder a moment, Enoch looks up and tells the driver it's seven minutes after four. In a flash the Cadillac pulls off down the road — but not without the driver wondering how Enoch knew so precisely the time of day by feeling that cow's udder.

Upon his return, though, the driver has become sufficiently intrigued that he stops again to inquire.

"Earlier you told me the time of day," the driver says.

"Yes," Enoch recalls, "While I was milking the cow."

"That's why I stopped," the driver says, "I'm really interested to know how you could determine the exact time simply by feeling that cow's udder.

"All I did was push it aside," Enoch tells him, "and I could see the steeple clock on the Congregational Meeting House down the Center."

The Center of Things

Vermont and New Hampshire are geographic opposites divided on the diagonal by the Connecticut River flowing south from a puddle in Québec. From the Vermont perspective, New Hampshire is the "upside-down state," though in New Hampshire the observation is naturally reversed.

That summer visitor who has a cabin up Moose Head Trail, the German fellah with the horse, he likes riding, and occasionally he rides across the river way up backcountry. On one of those times he came upon a distant farm where the farmer's out working his field.

"Don't you feel lonely way back here?" the German inquires from his place high in the saddle.

"I don't know what you're talking about," the farmer replies.

"I just thought maybe you'd want to be more near the center of things," the German says.

"I live exactly seven miles from Center Northwood and exactly seven miles from Rumford Falls," the farmer tells him, "and I am exactly one hundred, sixty miles from Boston and exactly one hundred, sixty miles from Montréal. I don't know how a fellah could be much nearer to the center of things."

Back From College

Roger Hancock's younger son, Kenny, is back from State College, and he's with his father in the barn when Enoch Webster stops over. As they shoot the breeze, Enoch, who is sort of supporting himself by leaning against a stanchion, has his eyes fixed on father and son as they do chores.

"How you like it up there to college?" he asks Kenny.

"Wicked good," he replies.

"What you studying?" Enoch inquires.

"Liberal arts, mostly," Kenny tells him.

"What's that?" Enoch wants to know.

"History, English, Science," Kenny replies.

"You getting good grades?" Enoch asks.

"Pretty good," Kenny tells him.

Enoch, who is some seventy years older than Kenny, watches a spell as the boy mucks stalls with his father — and remembers back when Roger in his younger days mucked stalls with his father, George.

"Good boy you got here," Enoch finally says, "College ain't hurt him a bit."

More Bull Troubles

Josiah's having trouble with that bull of his again. Seems now the critter's constipated, so Josiah goes down to see Enoch Webster. Enoch tells him to use a funnel and give that bull an enema using warm soapy water.

Josiah hasn't got a funnel, but during the war when he was in the Army, he was issued a bugle — they didn't want him carrying a gun. Ultimately, Josiah proved useless as a bugler, but he kept the bugle anyway.

Remembering this, Josiah fetches the bugle, fixed up a bucket of water, goes out to the field, and shoves that bugle up the bull's tail end.

Well, that bull decides right then and there not to hang around for the rest of the treatment. He kicks up and starts jumping around the meadow, but every time that bull jumps, he toots. Josiah's bull bounds over the stonewall then shoots up North Road a-jumping and a-tooting, a-jumping and a-tooting.

Along about that time Harold Cotter, the town constable, comes by. Hearing the racket, he assumes some of the boys from Northwood Academy were up the mountain causing a ruckus as they often do. Then he spots Josiah chasing that bull.

"What you looking at?" Josiah hollers at the constable.

"I thought some boys were up here raising hell," he shouts back.

"If you can't tell the difference between boys raising hell and a bull with a bugle up his ass," Josiah hollers, "You ain't fit to be constable!"

The Dog Died

Spud and Isabelle Carpenter, who have been away visiting family, are greeted by Junior Coates on the road into their farm. Junior's been watching the place while they've been away.

"How'd it go, Junior?" Spud asks through the car window.
"Not bad at all, considering," Junior tells him.
"Considering what?" Spud inquires.
"The dog died," Junior reports.
"What of?" Spud wants to know.
"Seems he got some bad well water," Junior replies.
"What happened to the well?" Spud inquires.
"When the chicken drowned," Junior says, "it tainted the well."
"How'd the chicken get into the well?" Spud asks.
"Probably confused by the flames," Junior says.
"What flames?" Spud wants to know.
"From the barn," Junior replies.
"What happened to the barn?" Spud inquires.
"It burnt," Junior tells him.
"What set it off?" Spud asks.
"Lightening, most likely," Junior says.
"Lightening struck the barn?" Spud asks him.
"Probably not," Junior replies.
"Then what set off the barn?" Spud inquires.
"Well, this is how I figure it," Junior says, "After the lightening hit the house, a spark flew and lit the barn scaring the chickens causing one of them to fall in the well, so when the dog drunked the water he got chicken poison and died. Other than that, it warn't bad at all, considering."

Too Much Arguing

It's come haying time and Enoch Webster's puts up a "Man Wanted" notice on the bulletin board down Bill Peterson's Country Store. In next to no time he hires a fellah, who's looking for work.

"Nice crop of timothy," the fellah says to him on his first day down to Enoch's. Then they didn't have occasion to say anything until supper.

"That's alfalfa," Enoch tells him at supper, and they don't say another word all night. The next morning, Enoch goes out to the barn to fetch the fellah, and he finds a note nailed to a stanchion.

"Left, too much arguing," the note says.

The Little Turkey

Some years back when Roger Hancock's older son, Joe, was just a child, Roger thought he'd better prepare him for the realities of farm life by giving him a little turkey to raise on his own.

The boy did a commendable job raising that bird, but the challenging part came when Roger tells him he'll have to kill and pluck it for Thanksgiving dinner. Unsurprisingly, Joe resists, but he does as his father orders and goes out to the pen with an ax.

After he'd gotten into the pen, though, the turkey stares at Joe, and Joe stares at the turkey, at it is at that moment he hatches a plot, hiding the turkey until Thanksgiving is over. Come Christmas, however, Roger isn't having anymore of this and demands Joe prepare the turkey for Martha to roast. But Joe's heart still isn't in it.

The afternoon of Christmas Eve, Joe goes into the pantry and fetches a jug of Barbados rum, figuring if he gets that turkey pickled, it will be easier for the both of them. Well, that turkey got drunk alright and flops right onto the ground, so Joe just takes the bird, plucks it, and sticks it into the icebox.

Christmas morning, Martha came down early, takes the turkey out of the icebox, sets it on the counter in the warmth of the cookstove, and in a matter of minutes that turkey came to and begins strutting around the kitchen, naked and hungover.

Well, Joe never did kill that turkey, and Roger reluctantly accepted that his exercise in farm life was a cause lost on Joe. So Martha, after hurriedly preparing a Christmas dinner of venison, spent the rest of the afternoon knitting a sweater for the turkey.

Bull Shooting

Godfrey mighty! Seems Josiah Coates is having trouble with that bull of his again; so he bicycles down to see Enoch Webster as usual. After Josiah explains the problem, Enoch gives him a pill and instructions to either feed it to the bull by mouth or by inserting it by tube through the tail end.

Since he'd caused so much commotion that last time, he reckons he'd best approach the problem from the front, but no matter how hard he tries, Josiah just can't get that critter to take down the pill. So, as sort of a last resort, he gets his youngest son, Jeremiah, over with his peashooter to fire that pill in using a rearward attack.

"I ain't blowing no pill up no bull's ass," Jeremiah says flatly.

"Why not?" asks Josiah, "Enoch says it'll work."

"Not if that sonuvabitch blows first," says Jeremiah.

Wore It Off

Enoch Webster is baling his new crop of alfalfa when a tourist pulls up to the gap in the stonewall, gets out of his car, then walks across the field toward Enoch.

"I'm sort of lost," he admits, "Would you mind telling me how to get to Snug Harbour?"

"Well, you went the wrong way out of Center Northwood," Enoch tells the tourist, "so you'll need to turn yourself around, pass back through the Center, then continue down through the notch to Salt Cove." All the while Enoch's pointing the way.

"I can't help notice," the tourist comments, "but the end of your finger's missing. What happened?"

"Oh, that happened a long time ago," Enoch tells him, "I wore it off pointing directions to tourists."

The headlands and Cod Point lighthouse.

17.
Wooden Ships & Iron Men

IN THE DAYS OF THE GREAT WOODEN SAILING SHIPS, one of the traditions among the "iron men" of the sea was to refer to their boats by the female pronoun. Many a mariner then and since has acknowledged, "She treats me better than any woman has."

Some fellahs even name their boats after their sweethearts, wives, daughters, or their homeport. Names like MARY ANN, SARAH & BETTY, and MISS GLOUCESTER are common on the New England coast. Our buddy, Tom, once captained a commercial fishing trawler called MISS PHYLLIS, though boys being boys she was known around her home port as "Miss Syphilis."

This isn't to suggest every vessel that takes to sea carries a female name — or any name at all for that matter. Each summer the Jamestown Yacht Club in Rhode Island is benefactor of a flotilla of nautical nonsense called the Fool's Rules Regatta, where some fifty contenders slap together in a mere two hours sailboats composed of no recognized nautical materials. Hull construction typically comprises bed frames, bathtubs, doghouses, hay bales, and car parts. Bed sheets, drapes, and tarps predictably serve as sails. In addition to getting soaked, competitors are awarded a range of prizes from "Most Ingenious Design" to "Worst Example of Naval Architecture".

☛ At the turn of the last century, a competition of a different sort was declared by financier J. Pierpont Morgan, head of the New Haven Railroad and its subsidiary, the Fall River Line, provider of steamship passenger and mail service between lower Manhattan and Fall River, Massachusetts with continuing rail service to Boston.

It seems that up Maine, Charles W. Morse, the "energetic son of Bath", then and now New England's great shipbuilding port, had gained control of Maine's steamship lines and had set his eyes on the lucrative Long Island Sound run. His plan was to provide faster, all-water service between Manhattan and Boston. This naturally threatens Mr. Morgan's monopoly and his plans to turn the route into an all-rail service.

To meet this competition straight on, Mr. Morgan quickly hires New Englander Charles S. Mellon from the Northern Pacific Railroad, and together with J. Howland Gardner, chief of the Fall River Line's Newport, Rhode Island shipyard, conspire to expand service by *both* land and sea.

Up to now the Fall River Line is known primarily for its elegant steamship, PRISCILLA, the "Jewel of Passenger Service" and described in *Marine Journal* as "a dream in naval architecture." But luxury isn't speed, and then as now everyone's in a hurry whether they need be or not. So the cry becomes "build bigger than PRISCILLA!" which they do.

At four hundred, fifty-six feet in length with a speed of twenty knots, COMMONWEALTH, the largest and fastest steamship ever to sail Long Island Sound, is launched in 1919 and quickly becomes the fashionable winner of what became known as "The War of Long Island Sound."

The New Punt

Although much Yankee humor originates inland, there's a whole other body of tales that come from the sailing and fishing traditions of coastal New England, particularly Downeast Maine, so called because to get there it's necessary to sail downwind, east from Boston.

Seth Thayer, before he died, used to live down Fairview Farm on Salt Cove. One summer his grandson, Luke, came down from

Center Northwood and stayed on until the start of school in the fall. Early most mornings Luke would untie his grandfather's punt from the dock out front of the farmhouse and row out to the seawall to fish then he'd scull around the cove looking for horseshoe crabs.

One morning right before he's about to go back, Luke stoves the punt on a rock, busting a hole in the starboard bow. Seth curses him something wicked and tells him to go home and never come back.

The following year when Seth calls for him to visit, Luke won't come and stays up the Center all summer. It's soon after that when Seth takes a fatal fall off his barn roof and dies.

Luke comes down to Charley Snow's funeral parlor with his folks for the service. After he walks in and sees Seth laid out there, Luke runs up to the coffin and looks right in.

"Hello, Grandpa," he says, "I see you built yourself a new punt."

Set Her Again

This story may be offensive to the fat folks among us, but you've got to realize upcountry there are some rather hefty citizens, spending winters as they do hibernating and exercising just their eating muscles. There's a saying, "The only difference between that fellah and a moose is fifty pounds and a flannel shirt."

Matt Conley's a lobsterman whose boat is named after his wife, Mary Ann. He has a hired hand, a young fellah named Tony Briggs, and all autumn they've been pulling lobster traps along the breakwall between Salt Cove and the Atlantic Ocean. Despite their best efforts, though, lobstering's off and money is tight.

Matt's mother-in-law had been visiting her sister out California and is just now returning home, so Matt and Mary Ann drive down to the depot in Rumford Falls to fetch her. Well sir, Matt's mother-in-law is one hefty woman who carries quite a lot of tonnage. "She's shade in the summer and warmth in the winter," her late husband used to tell folks.

"How'd you like California?" Matt asks as she steps off the train.

"It's alright," she replies, "but it's too far from the ocean." Since she'd been away all this time, she really wants Matt to take her out for "a little boat ride"; and since she's never been on a lobstering boat before, Matt really tries to talk her out of it, but she's persistent.

Well, the thing about women with tonnage is the more they ton, the more they talk, and she's pretty much talking the ears off Matt and Tony as they head out Salt Cove through the gap to pull traps. The sea smoke on the cove clears as they get to the ocean side, but it's wicked choppy, so that quiets her down some.

After they fetch about in the chop awhile, and Matt starts hauling the first of the string, Tony lifts the cover off the bait barrel, which has been setting in the sun since noon yesterday. The aroma gives Matt's mother-in-law kind of a greenish hue, and so as the boat eases closer to Cod Point, and the chop turns to swell, that old lady takes to the rail.

They'd been pitching side-to-side a spell when Matt happens to look around. "You seen my mother-in-law?" he shouts to Tony.

"I haven't seen her," Tony replies.

They circle back, following the string, but it's beginning to get dark, and soon they can't see a thing.

"Your wife's not going to be pleased," says Tony.

The next morning, Matt and Tony head out early to see if they can find his mother-in-law and to pull traps.

"Matt!" Tony shouts, after working the string, "It won't budge."

Matt goes aft from the wheelhouse, and together they tug until the trap clears the rail.

"I'll be damned," says Tony.

Draped over the trap is Matt's mother-in-law, and she's got a couple dozen lobsters clinging to her.

"What we gonna do?" Tony asks.

"The first thing we're gonna do is peg those lobsters," Matt tells him, "Then I suppose we should set her again."

All I Know

Relevant to this story is an item of boatyard equipment called a marine railway, which, as the name implies, is a set of standard railroad tracks that descends beneath the water and upon which a cradle hauls vessels ashore for hull repairs.

You remember that time Walt Palmer built the catboat for Dr. Robert Kenny, our town's physician? He named it BONITO, and in the time since, the good doctor's become quite a skilled sailor. In fact, he's usually out every Monday, which is his day off.

This one afternoon, though, Dr. Kenny is sailing alone when he notices a leak around the keel. He brings her in to Fish's Dock and looks around the best he can, but he can't find anything wrong.

Cap Clark, master of Clark's Boatyard in Salt Cove, is renowned for the exceptional wooden ships fabricated at his yard. He's also the fellah most everyone goes to for boat repairs, so Dr. Kenny figures he best sail over and have Cap diagnose it.

"Pull her up on the ways, Doctor," Cap tells him, "and we'll take look at it."

The boat slowly rises out of the harbor, and there's water dripping all around under the hull. Dr. Kenny kinda looks at it, but he still can't see where it's leaking. Cap, though, he goes right over and smells around, then signals his foreman.

"Put a little extra wood over there by the garboard, right at the starboard side by that beam there," Cap says, "Knock it through and get that dead wood out, and we'll have it done in about a half hour."

Then Cap goes over and sits on a nail keg and starts whittling on a piece of soft pine he has there.

"Captain Clark, that was truly marvelous," Dr. Kenny says, after walking over to him. "I just can't reckon how you knew that so quickly."

"Goddamit man," Cap says, "I can't understand all I know."

They're Crawling!

In order to conserve the stock, New England lobstermen are supposed to throw back any catch that doesn't meet government regulations. One of the culls that are supposed to be returned to the deep are "softs", molting lobsters whose new shells are still too soft to legally bring to market. The other are "shorts", lobsters whose tail joints are smaller than the legal size indicated on a brass gauge lobstermen carry.

As Matt Conley and Tony Briggs chug back toward Salt Cove tossing culls into the ocean, Tony retains a two-pounder, sticking it into his duffel to take home. After off-loading the day's catch at Fish's Dock, Matt hauls around and drops Tony off at the state pier.

Tony chucks his duffel onto the pier and is just about to jump onto the pier himself, when Ed Sweet, the fish warden, comes along.

"What y'got in the bag?" Ed wants to know.

"Just some dirty clothes", Tony tells him. Ed looks at the duffel bag, then looks back to Tony.

"You sure?" he asks.

"Yeah," says Matt, "Just some wicked dirty clothes."

"I'd say they're dirty," Ed comments, "They're crawling!"

Don't Want To Be Beholden

It's fairly unusual for sailors to speak of misfortune until trouble actually befalls — tragedy being the unspoken worry of many mariners all their days at sea. The weather-worn, salt-veiled Fisherman's Memorial at harbor side attests to that.

All the same, Walt Palmer and Tom Lillibridge put out for George's Bank, the rich fishing grounds off New England's coast, as they have so many times before. They're in Walt's fishing smack,

DAUNTLESS, and as usual they don't talk too much. "We're out there for fishing not chatter," is the way Walt puts it.

On this particular trip, as often happens, a thick fog settles in. This time, though, it doesn't lift, and there's no wind. As the day passes, they lose their bearings. Another day passes, and there's still no let up. A third day: their food's run out, and the drinking water's almost gone.

"We better do something," says Walt, "Or we're done."

"It'd take an act of God," Tom comments.

"I think we better pray to the Lord," Walt advises. They had just gotten down on their knees and are about to start, when Tom looks around and spots the steam packet COLUMBIA breaking through the fog off starboard.

"If you haven't said it, don't say it," he says to Walt, "We don't want to be beholden to anybody."

The Old Pilot Book

The boat of this story is a small cargo sloop called a "coaster", since it generally sails close to visible shoreline, carrying no navigational aids save coastal charts, a pilot guidebook, and good eyesight. The small foresail stretched on a wooden bowsprit is the jib, and the large aft sail stretched on a short gaff at the top and a longer spar at the base is the mainsail, or *munsul* in the jargon of coastal New England. Also, in this story is the old English word *hail*, meaning "to yell for", and the christening is a boat launching.

"Were you ever to down Snug Harbour?" Henry Foster asks the students at Northwood Academy. He's giving an oration to the assembly there. "That's where I was born and raised and lived there all my days, man and boy, following the sea. I ain't never done much blue water sailing, mostly coasting, and I got me a little sloop called the PILGRIM that me and my nephew, Raymond, run.

"We don't carry no hands, Ray and me, we really don't need no hands. We don't have no problem running her except for the munsul. The munsul's kinda heavy for Ray and me, so we don't often lower the munsul, just lower the jib and ease the peak and let the munsul flap mostly.

"Now, you'd think a fellah like me would know every mite of those waters like the back of my hand, but you never can tell. I recollect one time we were tied up to the state pier taking on a deckload of lumber for Rose Island.

"Well sir, at noontime we're ready to sail, so we ease away and hoist the jib. We didn't have to raise the munsul; we hadn't lowered the munsul. The munsul's kinda heavy for Ray and me, so we just lower the jib and ease the peak and let the munsul flap, like I said.

"When we get along past Cod Point lighthouse the hail on the headlands is shouting for us to come ashore; it seems they are having a hair-setting party, sort of a christening. There's six fathoms of water there under the head, so we run in close and drop the anchor and lower the jib. We don't often lower the munsul, so we ease the peak and just let the munsul flap mostly.

"When I tell you they have two barrels of Barbados rum jacked up, you'll know they're setting the baby's hair good and proper."

"You sure this is appropriate?" Mr. Johnson, the headmaster, whispers to Henry, "Given the circumstances."

"As I say," Henry continues, "After a spell Ray says to me, 'If we're ever gonna get that lumber out to Rose Island, we best get a-going', so we hoisted the jib. We didn't have to hoist the munsul; the munsul's kinda heavy for Ray and me, so we don't often lower the munsul, just lower the jib and ease the peak and let the munsul flap, you know.

"Well, we put away for Rose Island, but we ain't more than got out when comes in a fog so thick we can't hardly see a thing. We fetch back and forth for a spell without getting anywhere, so Ray asks me, 'Where are we, you suppose?'

"'Darned if I know,' says I, 'Why don't you go below and get me that pilot book, and we'll kinda figure it out.'

"Well, that pilot book's kinda old, and the binding's busted. I ain't hardly got it opened to the Cod Point to Rose Island page when a gust of wind comes up and blows that page plumb overboard.

"'Now what we gonna do?' asks Ray.

"'I'll tell you what we're gonna do,' says I, 'We're gonna get moving and get out of here and over onto this next page, then by golly we'll know where we be.'"

Hardly Got My Bait Back

As you probably know, Matt Conley and Tony Briggs, his hired man, run out through Salt Cove nearly every morning to tend a string of lobster traps along the breakwall. Well, Matt's wife, Mary Ann, she's expecting their first baby anytime now.

"If anything happens," Matt says to Joe Hancock, who works ashore, "I'd sure appreciate it if you'd come out and let me know."

"Yessah," Joe promises, "I'll tell you when it happens."

One morning Matt and Tony are out working the string when a fog closes in, which isn't all that unusual. Since they're already out to the breakwall, they figure to keeping hauling and baiting, which they do until they hear the bub-bub-bub of an outboard motor coming toward them in the fog.

"Who is it?" Matt hollers.

"You're a father!" Joe yells back, easing in slowly.

"What is it?" Matt wants to know.

"She's a girl," Joe says.

"How big?" Matt asks.

"Two pounds, ten ounces," Joe reports.

"Gawd," Matt comments, "I hardly got my bait back."

Walt On the Train

Walt Palmer, as you know, is a commercial fisherman who owns the smack DAUNTLESS. One evening he's laying on his couch reading *The Northwood Independent* and notices there's a fishing conference being held in Boston, so he decides to go down.

He's never been on a train before, so after he gets aboard at the Rumford Falls station, he sits down in one of those aisle seats when the conductor comes along.

"You can't leave that suitcase in the aisle like that," he tells Walt, "You better do something with it."

After a spell, the conductor comes by and nearly trips over the suitcase again.

"I thought I told you to do something with that," he says with a stern expression, "If I come by again and that suitcase isn't moved, I'll take care of it myself."

Walt is looking out the window at the farms and fields passing by when the conductor comes by again, but this time he doesn't say a word. He just picks up that suitcase, hauls it out onto the platform between carriages and heaves it out into a passing cornfield. Walt just sits there watching. After a spell the conductor comes back down the aisle again.

"That'll fix you," the conductor says to Walt, "How you like that?"

"I wouldn't have, if it had been mine," Walt replies.

The Headlands Have Sunk

"Cap Clark is a master shipwright and a master skipper, too," Henry Foster says, talking about his younger days when he served under Cap on the cargo schooner NONESUCH. In those days before navigational electronics, depth measurements were attained by lowering overboard a line with fathom marks on it and weighted by a lead sinker. It's from this "lead" that Samuel Langhorne Clemens took his pseudonym, Mark Twain, meaning "two fathoms", a depth considered safe for navigation.

"I will never forget that night passage when I was mate," Henry continues, "I went below to Cap, who was in his cabin with an attack of sciatica.

"'Captain Clark, we're too close to shore,' I tell him, 'The fog is thick, and the wind's fresh, and we're carrying too much canvas, so might I trim the sail?' Cap sets up and says to me, 'Sound and pass the lead below,' so I went on deck and heaved the lead.

"'Five fathoms with sand,' I report after returning below.

"'Pass me that lead,' Cap says, then with his finger he scrapes a mite of sand out of the hollow and sets it on his tongue. 'Don't you mean six fathoms, Mr. Foster?' he says me.

"'Six it is,' I reply, 'but I subtracted one for assurance.'

"'Rightly done,' says Cap, 'We're close in with the land and must remain prudent. Keep northeast, half east, straight as a rod, sort out the reef, and bring her in. If you don't hear breakers in fifteen minutes time, inform me of it.'

"In precisely fifteen minutes I could hear those breakers crashing on the headlands. 'Luff and shaker her,' I shout to the boys, and we bring her into the wind as the beacon of Cod Point lighthouse comes into sight.

"It is then I reckon to put Cap to the test, so I swing the lead and cast it ashore, then haul it aboard to take below.

"'Cap Clark,' I say to him, 'The fifteen minutes have passed, and it blows brisk and spits thick.'

"'Mr. Foster, you haven't kept this vessel straight,' says Cap, then he takes the lead, tastes the dirt, and spits it onto the cabin deck. 'There's no fault in your reckoning,' he tells me, 'but I regret to inform you that the headlands have sunk, and we're now over Seth Thayer's compost heap.'"

Matt's Baby

The morning after seeing his daughter for the first time, Matt Conley is puttering aboard his lobster boat, MARY ANN, when he spots Tony Briggs approaching down the dock.

"So how's the proud papa?" Tony yells as he jumps aboard. They're about to head out, as they do most every morning.

"The first thing Mary Ann wants to do,' Matt complains, "is get gussied up and go out celebrating."

"She wants to look nice," Tony says.

"Women today," Matt responds, "Their rigging's worth more than their hulls."

"And your daughter?" Tony inquires.

"I hate to find fault," Matt says.

"I bet," Tony replies.

"But if you handed me a stick of soft pine and a sharp knife," Matt tells him, "I could whittle you a better looking baby than the one I got."

Warm Water

Walt Palmer and Tom Lillibridge are out fishing aboard the smack DAUNTLESS, when Tom smells something burning. He looks around the deck, into buckets and on all sides of the canvas and rope piled on deck, but he still doesn't see anything. Then he starts sniffing around Walt.

"What the blazes you up to," he says to Tom.

"I smell smoke," Tom says, "and I think you're afire."

"No, I'm not," Walt says. It's a wicked cold day, and the wind's brisk.

"Check your pockets," Tom suggests, "It smells to me like tobacco plug."

"I ain't alit," Walt insists. Just to be sure, though, Tom lifts up the tail of Walt's slicker and the seat of his pants are all ablaze. Immediately, he grabs the sluice bucket, drops it over the side by its rope, then hauls the bucket up and empties it onto the seat of Walt's pants.

"Godfrey, Tom!" Walt hollers, "Where'd you get all that warm water?"

Index

Abbott, J. Stephen, 91
Abbott-Downing, 91
Adams, Samuel, 55
American Revolution, 55
Attucks, Crispus, 55

Barnstormers, 131
Barnum, P. T., 78, 129
Bean, Leon Leonwood, 140
Ben & Jerry, 38
Bert & I, 65
blue laws, 77
Borden, Lizzie, 56
Boston, 4, 11, 26, 30, 34, 67, 85, 113, 121, 126
Boston & Maine Railroad, 115, 145
Boston Brahmin, 11
Boston Post, The, 6, 27
Boston Red Sox, 113
Brook Farm, 46
Bryan, Robert, xvi, 65
burlesque, 121

Cardiff Giant, 129
cemetery, 55
Champ, 139
Christian Science, 68, 69
Clemens, Samuel Langhorne, 2, 91, 173
collywobbles, xix, 72
Combat Zone, 122

Concord Coaches, 91
Congregational Church, 45, 54
Connecticut, 11, 25, 67, 77, 78, 128, 130
Coolidge, Calvin, v, xix, 27, 28, 35, 37, 72
Curley, James Michael, 105

Danbury Fair, The Great, 130
de Champlain, Samuel, 139
dialects, 11
Dickenson, Thomas Newton, 68
Dodge, Marshall, xvi, 65
Downeast, 164
Downing, Lewis, 91

Eddy, Mary Baker, 68
Emerson, Ralph Waldo, 13, 19

Fall River Line, 162
Farmer's Almanac, 147
Foley, Alan, xv
Fools Rules Regatta, 161
Frank Jones Ale 85, 88
French and Indian War, 25
Frost, Robert, 1

Goose, "Mother" Elizabeth, 55
Granary Burial Ground, 55
Great Danbury Fair, The, 130

Hancock, John, 55
Harding, Warren G., xix, 72
Harvard College, 113

Harvard Lampoon, 113
Hasty Pudding Society, 113
Holmes, Oliver Wendel Sr., 113

Jackson, Gen. Thomas "Stonewall", 152
Jamestown Yacht Club, 161

Kennedy, John F., Presidential Library, 113
Kennedy, Joseph P. Sr., 83

Lake Champlain, 139
Leahy, Patrick, 78
Leno, Jay, 78
Loring drawings, cover, vi, 24, 64, 104, 138, 162
Loring, Paule, xxi
L Street Brownies, 105

Mayflower II, xxii
Maine, 11, 12, 25, 55, 128, 140, 164
Massachusetts, xix, 11, 13, 25, 27, 55, 56, 66, 67, 77, 78, 113, 128, 161
Model T, xix, 91
Moose, 140, 141, 142
Morgan, J. Pierpont, 161
Mount Washington Observatory, 106
Moxie, 3, 10, 37, 74, 94

Narragansett Lager, 85, 88
New England Fair, 128
New England, map of, xiv
New England Telephone Company, 69
New England Transcendentalism, 13

New England Unitarians, 45
New Hampshire, 11, 56, 77, 79, 106, 148, 154
New Haven Railroad, 161
Newton, Lon, 36

O'Brien, Conan, 78
O'Brien, John, 78
Old Howard, The, 121

Package stores, 83
patent medicines, 67
Pilgrims, 43, 45
Pinkham, Lydia, 67
Pitcher's Garage, xv
Ponzi, Carlo "Charles", 26
Powell, Thomas Reed, 1
Prohibition, 83
publick bills of credit, 25
Puritans, 45, 72, 121

Revere, Paul, 55
Rhode Island, xv, 11, 12, 25, 67, 77, 78

Scollay Square, 121
Shakers, 46
Sloan, Earl S., 67
songs, 149
State Store, 83, 84

Thayer, Henry, 68
Thoreau, Henry David, 13
tonic, xix
Trappist monks, 19

Tuttle, Fred, 78
Tuttle, Samuel A., 68
Twain, Mark, 2, 91, 171

Vermont, 11, 25, 36, 72, 139, 154

Wampanoag, 43
Winchell, Walter, 148
"World Record Wind", 106
WMUR-TV, 79
WSB-TV, 152

Yankee Doodle, 119
Yankee tin peddler, 35

New England Country Store Cookbook

...makes the ideal gift!

NEW ENGLAND COUNTRY STORE COOKBOOK *IS YANKEE TRADITION, CULTURE, AND HUMOR ROLLED INTO ONE DELIGHTFUL VOLUME.*

This definitive collection of New England recipes, drollery, and folklore has enough incisive wit to delight and offend nearly everyone. What's more, the **over 325 classic recipes** contained within its pages are consistent in format and clearly written making each recipe a snap to follow!

available from
amazon.com
and booksellers everywhere